Christian I. Hall

D1112756

MY BEST
FRIEND'S
BOYFRIEND

Especially for Girls® Presents

MY BEST
FRIEND'S
BOYFRIEND

Written by
Kate William

Created by
FRANCINE PASCAL

BANTAM BOOKS
NEW YORK • TORONTO • LONDON • SYDNEY • AUCKLAND

This book is a presentation of **Especially for Girls**®,
Newfield Publications, Inc. Newfield Publications offers
book clubs for children from preschool through high school.
For further information write to: **Newfield Publications, Inc.**
4343 Equity Drive, Columbus, Ohio 43228.

Edited for Newfield Publications and published
by arrangement with Bantam Books, a division of
Bantam Doubleday Dell Publishing Group, Inc.
Especially for Girls and Newfield Publications are federally
registered trademarks of Newfield Publications, Inc.

RL 6, IL, age 12 and up

MY BEST FRIEND'S BOYFRIEND
A Bantam Book / September 1992

Sweet Valley High is a registered trademark of Francine Pascal

Conceived by Francine Pascal

Produced by Daniel Weiss Associates, Inc.
33 West 17th Street
New York, NY 10011

Cover art by James Mathewuse

ISBN 0-553-29233-1

Bantam Books are published by Bantam Books, a division of
Bantam Doubleday Dell Publishing Group, Inc. Its trademark,
consisting of the words "Bantam Books" and the portrayal of a rooster,
is a Registered in U.S. Patent and Trademark Office and in
other countries. Marca Registrada.
Bantam Books, 1540 Broadway, New York, New York 10036.

Printed in the United States of America

OPM 0 9 8 7 6 5 4 3 2 1

One

"Surprise." A stack of pages thumped down in front of Elizabeth Wakefield at the lunch table. Elizabeth looked around to see Penny Ayala, the school paper's editor-in-chief, pushing a pencil behind her ear.

"Let me guess. You need these edited and proofed by ten minutes ago," Elizabeth said, riffling through the pages. The roar of a typical Sweet Valley lunch period filled the air around her.

"Something like that," Penny agreed. "Can you bring them back to the office at the end of this period?"

Elizabeth smiled. Deadlines always seemed to arrive too soon. "Sure," Elizabeth answered. "No problem."

"Thanks," Penny said, then turned and

1

walked away. Elizabeth pushed aside her lunch and dug around in her bag for a pencil.

"The supreme sacrifice," a mocking voice said from behind her.

"You know me," Elizabeth said to her identical twin sister, Jessica. "I live and breathe for our school newspaper." Her blue-green eyes sparkled with laughter.

"Well, honestly," Jessica said, slumping into a chair next to Elizabeth, "it's depressing to be linked to someone who works so much. I have my reputation to consider, Liz."

Elizabeth grinned. Jessica's reputation was based on a firm foundation of stylish clothes, cheerleading, and gossip, all held together with nail polish. It was as solid as a rock, and Elizabeth knew her twin had nothing to worry about: no one would *ever* mistake Jessica for the serious twin.

Elizabeth had always been the more responsible sister. She had been born on time; Jessica had been born four minutes late. By nature, Elizabeth was more thoughtful, more cautious, and more studious than her sister. It had been a goal of hers from second grade on to be a writer. Writing for the school paper, *The Oracle*, was only one way to hone her skills. In recent months, she had begun to submit articles to the local Sweet Valley newspaper and to the prestigious *Los Angeles Times*. If her work sometimes meant skipping a party, or canceling a trip to the beach, it was an acceptable cost. Though Elizabeth enjoyed playing as much as the next

2

person, she was perfectly willing to give up a lot for her work.

Jessica, on the other hand, was always perfectly willing to give up work for play. Eleven years of school had taught her that time was too precious to spend all of it on books and math problems. So she cheerfully devoted hours at a stretch to playing tennis, shopping with her friends at the mall, or hanging out with her boyfriend, Sam Woodruff, while he worked on his dirt bike. Her itchy feet had led her into many tricky situations over the years, but her good instincts had always led her out just in the nick of time. Unfortunately, her idea of the right time to back out of an adventure did not quite coincide with her twin sister's. It was one of the few reasons there was ever any friction between them.

In spite of their differences, however, there was a unique tie that kept them the best of friends. Because they were physically identical, from their perfect size-six figures and honey-blond hair to the dimples in their cheeks, it was easy for them to take each other's places. Covering for each other had attained the level of an art form with the Wakefield twins. Of course, Elizabeth usually had to be dragged into schemes kicking and screaming, but as Jessica often pointed out, it would all make juicy material for a novel someday.

Elizabeth chalked up her escapades with Jessica to experience. Being a writer meant getting involved, and with Jessica around, there was *always* something to get involved in.

"You missed a typo there," Jessica said, pointing at a page with the straw from her can of diet soda. "Oh, here come Amy and Lila."

"Hi, twins," Amy Sutton said cheerfully as she pulled out a chair. "Who's got some interesting news? The grapevine is withering from lack of dirt."

"Here's a news flash: Elizabeth is working again," Lila Fowler pointed out in her typically dry tone. "Doesn't she know you're allowed to relax a few minutes every day?"

Elizabeth smiled and continued reading. Out of the corner of her eye she noticed a number of other friends coming to the table to eat their lunches. The conversations swelled around her, but didn't interfere with her ability to concentrate.

"So what kinds of really interesting calls have you gotten on the hotline lately?" Jessica asked, leaning across the table toward Amy.

"Jess," Elizabeth said, snapping back into the present at the sound of her sister's voice, "you know that's supposed to be confidential."

"It is," Amy agreed. "I made a promise to keep everything I hear absolutely private."

Sometimes it seemed strange to Elizabeth that gossipy Amy Sutton volunteered at a teen hotline. *Discretion* and *privacy* weren't in Amy's natural vocabulary. But surprisingly, Amy was really very good at her job. She did, however, like to talk about the *fact* that she worked at the hotline, though she never discussed specific calls.

"It's really important that people know they get total privacy when they call," Amy explained a

4

bit pompously. "Project Youth just wouldn't work if callers thought we were blabbing their problems to everyone. You have to swear an oath in order to be part of our special team."

"Come on, Amy," Jessica said with a laugh. "You make it sound like the Pentagon."

"The job requires just as much security," Elizabeth said. She knew Amy wasn't exaggerating. She had recently done a series of articles about the Project Youth clinic and its teen Helpline. The phone service at the community center had been started recently with money contributed by various private sources. One local family, the Morrows, had given a generous donation in memory of their daughter, Regina. If only a teen hotline had existed sooner, Elizabeth thought, her friend Regina might have had someplace to turn to when she was in trouble. Because Regina had felt so alone after her breakup with Bruce Patman, she had fallen into a downward spiral that had led to her death from a fatal reaction to cocaine.

"Elizabeth is right," Amy insisted. "Lots of the kids who call are really messed up. The only way we can help them is if we take it all very seriously."

"Can't you even tell us in general, vague, nonspecific terms what some of the calls are about?" Jessica prodded.

"Look out, Amy," Lila said. "The Jessica gossip-digging machine is going to work on you."

"You know," said Denise Hadley, a senior, "I've been trying to get my friend Ginny to volunteer for the hotline."

"Why doesn't she?" Elizabeth asked.

Denise shook her head, sending her lustrous red hair swinging across her shoulders. "She says she wouldn't know what to say. But she's a great listener. I know her well, and that's one of her best qualities."

The fact that Denise Hadley and Ginny Belasca were close friends was a surprise to some people. Denise was outgoing, poised, elegant—and knockout beautiful. Ginny was shy and self-effacing, and seemed to dress with the hope that she would be invisible. Elizabeth had once thought that Denise liked to hang around with Ginny because the contrast between them made Denise even more strikingly attractive. But now that she knew them both a little better, she realized that there was a real friendship between them.

"There's always room for more volunteers at Project Youth," Amy said to Denise. "And we'd train her so she'd know what to say. Try to talk Ginny into joining. If she's interested, she can talk to me, or call Kathy Henry. She runs the show."

Jessica put an arm across Elizabeth's shoulders. "Don't worry. If absolutely necessary, Liz will step in and help out. Just blow the trumpet and yell: 'Elizabeth Wakefield to the rescue!' "

Everyone around the table laughed. "At least Elizabeth takes her responsibilities seriously," Denise reminded Jessica. "Unlike some people."

"Uh-oh, low blow," Lila drawled.

"I consider it my responsibility making Sweet Valley High a more fun and exciting place to be,"

Jessica announced grandly. "And *that* is a job I take very seriously."

Elizabeth let out an exaggerated sigh of relief. "Well, thank goodness for that. That's one less thing for me to take care of. Now I can finish these and get them back to the office."

She stood up and waved goodbye to everyone. "See you later," she said. She smiled at Denise. "I hope Ginny joins the hotline."

"I'll keep working on her," Denise answered. "I promise."

"How does this color look on me?" Denise asked later that afternoon at the mall. She met Ginny's eyes in the mirror and raised her eyebrows.

Ginny ignored her own reflection and instead studied the effect of the emerald-green beret against her friend's shiny red hair. She smiled. "It looks great, of course."

"Should I get it?" Denise went on, tucking her hair up under the hat for a new effect. "I could wear it when I go to the concert tomorrow night with Jay."

"Poor guy," Ginny teased. "He'll be so busy looking at you, he won't hear a thing."

Denise plucked the beret off her head and swatted Ginny with it playfully. "Ha ha. Jay and I have been together so long, he doesn't even notice me anymore. I'm just as familiar to him now as his basketball sneakers. You know, important, but not something to sit around admiring every day."

"Yeah, right." Ginny shook her head. She knew as well as anyone that Jay McGuire didn't take Denise for granted. He had even confided to Ginny that sometimes he couldn't believe a beautiful, glamorous senior like Denise would go out with a lowly junior like him. Of course, he tended to overlook the fact that he was drop-dead handsome himself. But that was the effect Denise had on people: her beauty made people forget their own attractiveness.

In her own case, Ginny realized, there wasn't much to forget. She knew she wasn't pretty, and that was a fact she had always accepted, like any other fact of nature. The sun rose and set each day, and Ginny Belasca was mousy and easy to miss in an empty room. Paper-bag-colored hair, ordinary face—nothing special, straight down the line.

"Try this one on," Denise suggested after putting the beret back on the counter. She took a black fedora off the hatrack and held it out.

"Oh, please," Ginny said, waving it away.

"Come on, it's cool," Denise insisted as she placed it on Ginny's head. "I can never get you to try anything on."

Ginny took the hat off and put it down firmly. "That's because you always want me to try on things I would never wear. That hat is definitely *not* me."

"I'll see if I can find one of those clear plastic

hats, then," Denise said with a grin. "The kind old ladies wear."

"Mmm, that's perfect."

Ginny grinned. Sometimes Denise was very pushy, but it was all done out of love and friendship, and Ginny appreciated the intention. So they played out the same game over and over: Denise tried to talk Ginny into doing something, and Ginny stepped neatly out of the way. It had been that way for years, ever since they had first met at summer camp.

Ginny knew that lots of people, at first, wondered what their friendship was based on. At least they wondered why Denise would be friends with Ginny. But Ginny knew that she brought her share to their friendship. She knew she was smart, and pretty good at sorting through difficult problems; her self-mocking attitude toward life allowed her to see humor in many otherwise depressing situations. And although most of the popular girls at school only heightened Ginny's sense of insecurity, Denise never did. Denise had proved to be a true friend.

Ginny smiled at what she knew was going through her friend's mind at the moment. Denise was eyeing the hatrack critically.

"Deniiiiiiise," Ginny said. "It's not worrrrrking."

"But you'd look so pretty in some of these," Denise pleaded.

Ginny took her friend's arm and steered her away. "Forget it. I'm not pretty, so what's the point in dressing me up?"

"You *are* pretty," Denise said stubbornly.

"I am *not* pretty," Ginny said just as stubbornly.

"You have great inner beauty," Denise insisted. "And a beautiful voice, and—"

"And someday my prince will come," Ginny said. "Drop it, OK? My shopping tolerance is wearing thin and if you're not careful, I'll just leave."

Denise smiled ruefully. "Oh, all right. I just think if you *tried* a little harder . . ." she said quietly.

Ginny stopped and gave Denise a hard look. The one discussion that she really didn't want to slog through yet again was the issue of her datelessness. Denise was always wishing that she and Jay could double-date with Ginny and—and someone. But Ginny's shyness was an obstacle, and it really was too painful for her to discuss. She wasn't good at flirting, or even at carrying on a simple conversation with a boy she liked. She made so little impression on boys that they hardly knew if they had ever spoken to her. That was another fact of nature. Period.

"OK," Denise muttered. "I won't say another word."

"Until tomorrow, probably," Ginny said with a smile. "Do you want to go back and buy that beret?"

"Yes." Denise linked her arm with Ginny's, and they headed back to the hat display. "You know, I was talking about you at lunch."

Ginny cocked one eyebrow skeptically. "Oh really?"

"Some people were talking about the Project Youth hotline," Denise explained. "Have you thought any more about it?"

"Well . . ." Ginny leaned her elbows on the counter. "I know I'm not impressive in person, but I guess I do have a nice voice. Maybe people would feel like talking to me on the phone, when they can't see my dreary face."

"Ugh!" Denise groaned. "Get an attitude adjustment!"

Ginny shrugged. "I *have* been thinking, and I think I'll at least call to get some more information."

Denise grabbed Ginny's shoulders, and her brown eyes sparkled with delight. "You will? That's great! You'll be perfect, I know. Amy Sutton said the person to talk to is Kathy Henry. Call her when you get home, OK?"

"OK, OK!" Ginny chuckled. "You know," she admitted, "if I didn't have you around to push me, I probably wouldn't do anything at all!"

Two

Jessica pulled open the heavy front door of the building that housed the Project Youth program and stepped inside. A few teenagers were sitting together at one side of the waiting room, talking quietly. Jessica glanced at the clock on the wall. Since she never bothered to wear a watch, she never knew what time it was, and now she was startled to see she was actually early to meet Amy. With a shrug, she sat down in an easy chair and picked up a magazine from the nearby table.

She flipped through it impatiently. Being early didn't mean she was prepared to wait.

"Hi, can I help you?" a woman asked. "I'm Kathy Henry."

Jessica looked up with a quick smile. "Oh, I'm not a client or anything. I'm just waiting for Amy Sutton. We're going shopping when she's done with her shift. Can I go inside and wait for her?"

"Sorry," Kathy said. "The switchboard is off limits, but I'll let her know you're here."

"Thanks." Kathy walked through a door marked Private, and Jessica continued to flip through the pages of the magazine.

It still surprised Jessica that Amy was so serious and closemouthed about her work. Originally, Amy had been pressured into the job as a way of bringing up her sociology grade. But to everyone's amazement, Amy had found real rewards in the volunteer work. She had also met a fantastic boy, Barry Rork, who became her boyfriend.

Amy spent at least two afternoons a week answering phones in the next room. To Jessica, behind that tantalizing door labeled Private was a gold mine of interesting stories. It annoyed her that she could never pry any of them out of Amy. Amy knew full well that her friend had more than her share of natural, healthy curiosity!

"Oh, Jess, hi," Amy said, popping her head around the door. She looked flustered and upset. "I'll be—I just have to—"

"What's wrong?" Jessica stood up. "You look awful."

Amy threw a slightly desperate look over her shoulder and then seemed to come to a decision. "I have to take a break for a minute," she said to someone behind her. Then she came out into the waiting room and threw herself into another easy chair.

13

"So tell me what's wrong!" Jessica pressed.

"Oh, I don't know." Amy sighed. "I like working on the hotline, but sometimes I get so stressed out about the callers' problems."

"But they're total strangers," Jessica said. "Do you want to talk about it? I mean, pretend you're calling and I'm the one listening," she suggested.

"I shouldn't, but I'm so angry—so *outraged* . . ." Amy rested her forehead on her hand. She lowered her voice. "I just spent half an hour listening to this girl. Don't ask me what school she goes to, because I'm not saying," she added quickly.

"I won't," Jessica said, leaning closer.

Amy's slate-gray eyes were dark with suppressed emotion. "She's being harassed by one of her teachers," Amy began.

"What? You mean her grades are slipping?" Jessica prompted.

"No, I mean he's coming on to her," Amy whispered fiercely.

A slightly sick feeling settled in Jessica's stomach.

"She thought it was all in her imagination," Amy went on, shaking her head. "But she told me some of the details of what's been happening, and asked me what I thought. I told her it sounded as if her teacher was taking advantage of the teacher-student relationship, assuming she'd be too scared or confused to say anything to anyone."

"That's awful," Jessica said.

"It's *sick*. The girl was freaking out. She didn't

know what to do, where to go." Amy's voice cracked. "I felt so—so—I wanted to kill him."

Jessica sat back. To think of a *teacher* behaving that way with a girl who trusted him, making her feel so confused and ashamed and frightened—it *was* sick.

"Listen, I can't talk about it anymore," Amy said tiredly. "I really shouldn't have said anything at all. And Jess—I'm sorry, I don't feel like going shopping right now. I'll get a ride home later. I'm going to stay here for a while."

"I'm totally bummed out, too," Jessica muttered. She stood up and hitched her bag over her shoulder.

Amy nodded. "OK. Sorry."

"Don't be," Jessica answered. She trudged across the waiting room and opened the door. As she did, someone coming in bumped into her. "Oh, sorry, Jenny," Jessica said.

"It's Ginny," Ginny Belasca replied with a blush.

"Right. Sorry."

Ginny watched as Jessica made her way out to the street. Popular girls like Jessica Wakefield made Ginny feel even more insecure than usual. For them, talking to boys—talking to *anyone*—was as easy as falling off a surfboard. Denise was always trying to get Ginny to eat lunch with her and Jessica, or Lila, or the cheerleaders, but Ginny just couldn't do it. She was simply too intimidated by them. With Denise, it was different. She knew Ginny, and Ginny could be herself with her. But as far as the Jessicas of this world were concerned, Ginny tried to keep her distance.

Swallowing her nervousness, Ginny continued through the door. The first person she saw was Amy Sutton. Ginny cringed under a fresh wave of intimidation. But a moment later, Ginny's common sense took over, and she realized that if Amy was a volunteer here, there had to be an open, welcoming side to her.

"Hi. Um, I'm supposed to meet Kathy Henry," Ginny said shyly.

Amy looked at her blankly, and then shook her head. "Oh, right, Ginny. You're starting today?"

"I spoke to Kathy on the phone. She said to stop by this afternoon," Ginny explained.

"Hang on, I'll get her," Amy said.

While Amy went to find the director, Ginny examined her surroundings. The waiting room was warm and inviting. Posters covered the walls and comfortable chairs were scattered around the room. A rack of pamphlets stood by one window; titles such as "Dealing with an Alcoholic Parent" and "Coping with Stress" leaped out at her. She gripped the shoulder strap of her bag more tightly and wondered if she was doing the right thing, if she was really up to this kind of work.

"Ginny? I'm Kathy. It's nice to meet you."

As soon as Ginny turned around and saw Kathy Henry, her anxiety began to fall away. Kathy had an aura of calmness and understanding

16

about her that put Ginny at ease from the start. "Hi," she said. "Well, I'm here."

"Great. Let's sit for a few minutes and I'll explain how all this works," Kathy suggested, gesturing toward two chairs. "We've got a total of four hours of training for you to go through. We'll give you tips on how to listen effectively and tell you what kinds of other counseling agencies exist in the area so that you can steer a client in the right direction. And we'll tell you how to preserve your sanity! That sort of thing."

Ginny smiled. "It sounds reassuring," she said.

"You'll have your first hour of training now, and then you'll sit at the switchboard with a coach," Kathy explained. "Your coach will listen in on your calls, and be there as a backup."

"That sounds great," Ginny said. When Kathy stood up to lead the way into a private office, Ginny jumped up eagerly. She was ready to start.

For the next hour, Kathy and Ginny performed role-playing exercises. Kathy, as the caller, expressed different forms of anger, confusion, fear, and sadness. Ginny, in turn, tried to find a way to cut through each emotion and to get the caller to talk. Kathy then pointed out all the positive things Ginny had done and said, and also suggested possible alternatives. Even though Ginny was always aware that Kathy was acting a part, she still felt good as she tried to support and reassure, and to draw out the ideas behind the emotions.

When the hour was over, Kathy led Ginny into the switchboard room.

"You know Amy Sutton, right?" Kathy said. "And this is Barry Rork."

Ginny nodded shyly. She knew Barry was Amy's boyfriend, but she had been in a few classes with him and knew that he wasn't the kind of arrogant boy who made her completely tongue-tied.

"Hi," Barry said in a friendly voice. "I'm going to be your coach."

"He was my coach when I started," Amy said. She smiled warmly. "He's the best. I'm leaving now, so good luck."

"Thanks," Ginny said. She looked nervously at the switchboard and headsets and wondered how she would ever have the presence of mind to keep it all straight in her head.

"Relax," Barry said after Kathy and Amy had left the room. "It looks weird, but believe me, it's a piece of cake using this thing. Messes up your hairdo, though," he joked.

"Trust me, I'm not worried about that," Ginny said with a trace of her usual wryness. She sat down and listened carefully while Barry explained how to operate the lines.

"Got it?" he asked finally.

"I think so," she said.

"Good. I'll listen in on your first couple of calls."

Ginny put on the headset. Just then, a red light began flashing under one of the buttons. She glanced at Barry and he nodded for her to go ahead. Ginny pressed the button.

18

"Hello, this is Project Youth," she said. Her voice was calm and gentle, in spite of her fluttering stomach.

"Hi, my name is Valerie," a young girl said. "I don't know who to talk to."

"You can talk to me," Ginny said softly. "Are you worried about something?"

She saw Barry smile and nod at her. She was doing fine—so far.

"It's just that I was supposed to go to this party," Valerie said. "But my grandma's seventieth birthday is the same day, and my mom says I have to be with the family."

Ginny frowned. "Are you upset because you can't go to the party, or because your mother doesn't want you to go?"

"I don't know," Valerie complained.

"Well, let me ask you this. How do you feel about your grandmother?"

"Grandma? I love her more than anyone," Valerie said passionately. "She's so special to me. And I *do* want to be with her on her birthday," she added after a short pause.

"Maybe that's what matters most right now," Ginny said slowly. "It would be too bad if that fact got lost in the arguments with your mom."

"Well . . . that's true. And it's probably not even going to be such a hot party," Valerie admitted.

Ginny and Barry exchanged a smile. "So . . . ?" Ginny said to Valerie.

"So, I'll go to my grandmother's because I want to, not because my mother says I have to."

19

"It might help if you try to explain that to your mother," Ginny said. "Get her to see your point of view. Have you tried that before?"

"No, but I will. Thanks. I feel so much better!" Valerie sighed with relief.

"Call anytime," Ginny said. Then she cut off the line, sat back, and let out her breath. "Whoa."

"That was great," Barry said, giving her a thumbs-up sign. "Really nice."

"You have to admit, it was a pretty simple problem," Ginny countered.

"There aren't any simple problems, Ginny. Not for the kids who are having them."

"That's true," Ginny said, tapping her finger against her chin in a habitual gesture as she thought over the conversation. "Are you supposed to feel this good after listening to someone's troubles?"

Smiling, Barry tipped his chair back on two legs. "It does feel good, doesn't it?"

"It's great," Ginny continued. "You don't have to worry about whether the person likes you, or if you're making a good impression, or anything like that. You can just concentrate on the conversation and on the other person and be yourself."

"It can be pretty addictive," Barry agreed.

Another phone line began to flash. Ginny adjusted her headset quickly and hit the button. "Hi, this is Project Youth. What's on your mind?" she asked as Barry pressed down an extension button to listen in.

20

There was a long silence. Frowning, Ginny adjusted her headset again. "Hello? Are you OK?"

The person at the other end took a long, shuddering breath. "I—I don't know what to do," a boy said in a choked voice. "I'm just going out of my mind."

Ginny looked anxiously at Barry. This caller sounded seriously upset, and she thought someone with more experience should talk to him, but Barry simply nodded to her to continue.

"Listen," she said soothingly. "Can you start by telling me your name? You don't have to, but—"

"Mike. It's Mike," he said.

"Mike, can you try to tell me why you're so upset? Just a little bit at a time. You can stop whenever you want," Ginny promised.

"OK. OK, I'll try." Mike took a deep breath. "See, I just moved here two weeks ago. I go to Big Mesa High now."

"Mmm-hmm," Ginny murmured. Big Mesa was one of Sweet Valley High's main rivals. "Is it a problem at school?"

"No! It's not," he almost shouted. "Sorry, I didn't mean—"

"It's OK. You can shout at me if you want." Ginny looked quickly at Barry, and he nodded again.

"I'm really not crazy," Mike said, managing a faint, small laugh. "OK. Here's the story. My father . . . he—he died two years ago from cancer. We didn't find out he was sick until—" He broke

21

off, obviously trying to bring his emotions under control.

"I'm sorry," Ginny said softly, her heart going out to this boy who until a moment ago had been a complete stranger to her. She hoped she would find the right things to say.

"Then, six months ago," Mike went on, "my mother told me she was getting married. And I didn't even know she was *dating* anybody. She was keeping it a secret."

"Maybe she thought it would hurt you if you knew," Ginny suggested gently.

"Yeah, well, it hurt even more to find out that way. Suddenly she was making wedding plans, and I'm getting introduced to Joe—my step-father—and his two kids. It was like a nightmare. It happened so fast, and it was like it wasn't even *me* going through all the motions, you know?"

"I know," Ginny said. A painful rush of memories swirled through her, but she kept focused on Mike.

"Then we moved here. New family, new town, new school—I can't take it. I don't even know where I am or what I'm doing half the time. And Joe—I just can't do anything right, according to him. He thinks I should get a job after school instead of joining the track team, because *his* kids have jobs. He's always comparing me to them, always trying to boss me around. And my mother is always on his side! I just can't take it anymore! I won't!" Mike's last words came out in a tumbling, angry rush.

"What do you mean 'you won't'?" Ginny asked quickly.

There was a pause. "Nothing," Mike said glumly. "Forget it."

Ginny had seconds to make a decision. She had a hunch that Mike might be planning something desperate, but he clearly wasn't ready to confide that much. She could either push him to tell her what it was, or try to build his trust so that he would tell her on his own. She decided to treat him gently.

"Let me tell you what happened to me," Ginny said, her eyes scanning the room as her memories flooded back. "My father died when I was ten, and my mother got remarried a few years later. It was hard for me, but you know, I think it was hard for all of us. Trying to figure out what this new family was, how it works . . . it's tough, believe me. But we talked about it a lot, and that helped. Eventually, we worked it all out."

"Really?" Mike sounded hopeful.

"Try talking to your mother first," Ginny said. "If she didn't tell you about Joe when they were dating, it was probably only to protect you. You might have been afraid Joe would try to take your father's place, and maybe she thought she could save you from that pain. Maybe she didn't realize it had the opposite effect, that it made you feel powerless and betrayed."

"I don't know . . ." Mike said reluctantly.

"Have you tried to talk to her about your feelings? And ask her what her feelings are?" Ginny went on.

23

"No, not really," Mike confessed. "Maybe I haven't really tried hard enough."

"Give it a shot, OK?" Ginny said. "You have nothing to lose, right?"

"That's for sure," Mike said bitterly. He sighed. "I feel—I'm not sure what I feel, actually. But thanks. You've been great."

Ginny smiled, and felt tears of sheer relief come to her eyes. "That's what we're here for. Call back after you talk to her. The line's always open."

"But when do *you* work there?" Mike asked. "If I call back, I want to talk to you. I can't explain it all over again."

"I'll be here on Wednesday," Ginny said.

"I'll call on Wednesday. Thanks. Oh, what's your name?" he asked with a startled laugh.

She smiled again, feeling an incredible rush of happiness and confidence. "My name is Ginny."

"Ginny. Thanks again."

Feeling utterly weary and utterly elated, she took the headset off and stretched her arms.

Thanks for pushing, Denise, she said privately. *Thanks.*

Three

Denise wearily closed her math book and leaned back against the bleachers. The echoing *thud-thud* of the basketball and the short, sharp squeaks of the boys' sneakers filled her ears. Denise watched Jay run into the net for a lay-up; then she glanced at the clock. Practice was supposed to be over soon, but Denise knew that the coach sometimes kept the team late. She had plans to study with Ginny after dinner, but she hoped to talk to Jay before she left for home. During basketball season, most of his time was taken up with games and practices, and she felt that they hadn't had a conversation in ages.

It was getting late. She stood up.

"You're not leaving, are you?" Jay asked, running over to her.

"Well, I do have other things to do besides *watch*

you all the time," Denise said, smiling down at him from her perch at the top of the bleachers.

Jay was panting hard from practice. His sandy hair was wet and tousled, and his eyes sparkled. "Did you see that last lay-up?" he asked.

"Yes, it was perfect, stupendous, incredible," Denise replied, shouldering her bag and climbing down the steps. She sighed forlornly when she joined him at the bottom. "When are you going to be done?"

"Well . . ." Jay breathed deeply and looked over at the rest of the team. "I'm not sure. I'll call you later, OK?"

"OK," Denise said. "But Jay? Let's do something together tomorrow."

Jay glanced at the team again. "Uh . . ."

"Don't you have any time for me anymore?" Denise asked playfully.

Jay made a slight grimace. "You know I'm in training, Den. You understand."

"Yeah, I understand." Denise tried not to sound too impatient.

"We'll do something," he said quickly. "I have to go now. Bye."

"Bye." Denise followed him with her eyes as he ran back onto the court. She had the unpleasant suspicion that he had forgotten her the moment his back was turned.

Elizabeth sank back into the couch and propped her feet up on the coffee table in front of her. "Thanks for getting the ice cream," she said to her boyfriend, Todd Wilkins.

"No prob," he replied, groping underneath a cushion. "Where's the—I got it," he said. He fished out the remote control and turned on the television.

"What's on?" Jessica asked as she sauntered into the room.

"At the moment, we're coasting," Elizabeth said.

Todd continued to skim through the channels, pausing for a few seconds on each one. For an instant, they saw a teacher standing in front of a blackboard in a deserted classroom, leering down at a pretty, dark-haired student who looked up at him uncertainly. Todd flicked to the next channel.

"Ugh!" Jessica flung herself into an easy chair and made a horrible, sour face. "That show just reminded me. I've just *got* to tell you guys something," she announced.

Elizabeth rested her hand on Todd's to prevent him from switching from the nature program on the screen. She smiled. Animal behavior in the wild couldn't hold a candle to Jessica's behavior at home. They had their *own* wild kingdom whenever Jessica was around.

"OK, what is it?" she asked.

Jessica's eyes were stormy. "I was at Project Youth this afternoon, waiting for Amy? And she comes out, right? All upset?"

"Stop ending sentences on a question?" Elizabeth begged.

"Listen, this is serious," Jessica said firmly.

"She had a call from a girl at some high school who said a teacher of hers is coming on to her."

"What?" Elizabeth cried. "Wait a minute. Amy's not supposed to say anything about—"

"Well, she *did*. She was so upset, she had to vent her feelings a little," Jessica said, waving aside Elizabeth's objection. "And she didn't give any specific details. But that's not the point. The point is, it's just horrible that this poor girl is the victim of sexual harassment. Think about it—you wouldn't know if you were getting good grades because he liked you, or because you were earning them."

"I think worrying about grades would be the least of the girl's problems," Todd pointed out.

"I think it's disgusting," Elizabeth said indignantly. "It makes me feel like punching something."

"All I can say is, it's totally gross and barbaric," Jessica stated. "Change the channel, OK? This is boring."

Elizabeth stood up abruptly. "I need some fresh air."

She left the room and went out the back door to the patio. After a moment, she heard Todd walk out behind her. They stood in silence for a few moments, listening to the water lap and gurgle against the sides of the pool.

"Are you OK?" Todd asked at last.

"Yes," Elizabeth answered. "It just got to me. That poor girl. If it's true, she must be going through a lot of pain."

Todd slipped an arm across her shoulders. His special brand of sympathy and understanding was just one of the things that Elizabeth loved about him. He always knew when she needed a good listener.

"And if it *isn't* true, and she wrongly accuses her teacher," Elizabeth continued slowly, "that would be pretty rotten."

"Like what happened to Mr. Collins," Todd said, referring to the school's most popular teacher and advisor for *The Oracle*.

"Right," Elizabeth said, watching the pattern of reflected light dappling the branches overhead. "When Suzanne Devlin told everyone he had made a pass at her, he nearly lost everything: his job, custody of his son, his reputation. It nearly ruined his life."

Todd leaned against the edge of the picnic table. "Most accusations of sexual harassment aren't false, though."

"I know," Elizabeth said. "And that's why hearing about it gives me the creeps."

"There's nothing you can do," Todd reminded her gently. "Try not to lose perspective."

Elizabeth began to pace. "I know, I know. Sometimes I wish I didn't see so many of the things that make me mad, but when you write for a newspaper, you're *supposed* to see them. You're *supposed* to go looking for them."

"Are you surprised that you don't like what you find?" Todd asked.

"No."

"And you always end up pointing out the injustice to everyone else, too," Todd teased her gently.

Elizabeth shook her head. "I know. But I can't help

29

it. When I see something that's unfair or stupid or harmful, like beauty pageants, where women are displayed and judged like cattle—"

"Don't start on that again, please," Todd begged.

"Sorry." Elizabeth smiled at Todd in the darkness. "I just feel strongly about these things, you know that."

Todd reached for her and gave her a hug. "I know."

Elizabeth did feel strongly about unfairness. And hearing that a girl—who was probably a lot like Elizabeth or any of her friends—was being sexually harassed by a teacher made Elizabeth sick at heart. It also made her burn to do something about it.

"Do you suppose anything like that happens at our school?" she asked, tipping her head back to look up at the stars.

"I don't know," Todd admitted. "It's not the kind of thing you expect to see. And if it is there, you wouldn't necessarily notice it."

"Unless you were on the receiving end," Elizabeth said. "And even then, you might not really *understand* what you were seeing or hearing."

They were silent for a few moments. "There *is* something I can do about it," Elizabeth said finally.

"Such as?"

"I can write an article," she announced. "I want girls to be aware of what can and *does* happen in high schools, and tell them what they can and *should* do if they believe they're being harassed. I can tell them not to be afraid to tell someone."

"Another crusade?" Todd asked. "You take these things so hard, Liz. Don't do it if it's going to hurt you."

Elizabeth smiled and shook her head. "I'll try not to get so wrapped up in the story this time," she promised. She stepped close to him again and put her arms around his neck. "I'll be cool, detached, and objective."

"Sure," Todd said. "The reason you're such a good reporter is that you care. Just try not to care *so* much."

"I will," Elizabeth said. "At least, I'll try."

Ginny sat down at the Hadleys' dining room table with two glasses of orange juice. "Here," she offered, handing one to Denise.

"Thanks." Denise looked up from her homework with a swift smile. "I hate to ask this, but can you quiz me on these geometry rules?"

"Sure." Ginny pulled the sheet of paper toward her and ran through them for her friend. She only gave half her mind to the subject, though. She was remembering her afternoon at Project Youth, and especially her conversation with Mike.

I hope I was able to help, she thought. After all, it had only been her second call. She was not experienced the way Barry was. The one thing that held any hope for her was Mike's promise to call on Wednesday.

"What's wrong?" Denise asked. "You haven't caught me on one mistake."

"Oh, sorry." Ginny shook her head. "It's this Project Youth thing."

Denise smacked her forehead with one hand. "Oh, no! I can't believe I forgot to ask you about that! You must think I'm so selfish!"

"Don't be dumb," Ginny said fondly.

"So, tell me everything," Denise prompted with a smile.

Ginny rested her chin in her hand. "First of all, thanks for talking me into it. I really felt good about today. Except . . . Forget it," she said, waving her hand dismissively.

"No, tell me. What's wrong?" Denise said.

Ginny frowned. The most important thing about being a volunteer on the hotline was keeping everything confidential. Still, she thought she could discuss the situation in a general way with her friend. She trusted Denise completely.

"OK, here's the deal," Ginny said as Denise smiled at her encouragingly. "My second call was from a boy who was really upset about his home life. I'm pretty sure he was about to do something—run away or get into trouble—I don't know."

"And you talked him out of it," Denise said.

Ginny wrinkled her nose. "Well, that's what I'm not so sure about. We talked for a pretty long time, and he was a lot more relaxed at the end."

Denise leaned back in her chair and shook her head slowly. "I knew it. I knew you'd be great at helping people. You turned that guy around."

"I don't *know* if I did or not," Ginny insisted.

"But you said yourself he was much more re-laxed," Denise pointed out. "That's the main thing, right? To get someone to let off steam so he doesn't blow up?"

"That's true," Ginny agreed.

Denise picked up her orange juice and took a sip. "I can see how you'd be worried, though. I mean, you'll never know how it turns out."

"Well, actually," Ginny said, "he promised to call back Wednesday afternoon and tell me how it's going."

Denise's eyes gleamed. "Oh, really? Do I detect a budding friendship here?" she teased lightly.

Ginny blushed. "Oh, please, Denise. That's all you ever think about. He just doesn't want to have to explain the whole story to someone new when he calls again."

"You never know where these things can lead, though," Denise went on.

Ginny balled up a sheet of scrap paper and threw it at Denise. "For your information, phone counselors never meet the callers. It's strictly a first-name-only operation."

"So what does he sound like? Does he seem like a nice guy?" Denise asked.

"Ugh!" Ginny moaned. "You never give up, do you? He was too busy having a crisis for me to tell if he was a nice guy, OK?"

Denise nodded. "I'm sorry," she said sincerely.

"Don't worry about it." Ginny pulled her homework toward her and bent over it with an attitude of concentration.

But inside, she was thinking about Mike and

about how she was looking forward to his call on Wednesday.

"You will tell me what happens when he calls back, won't you?" Denise asked suddenly. Her smile told Ginny that her matchmaking thoughts were long forgotten.

"I will," Ginny promised. Then she crossed her fingers surreptitiously. "If he calls."

On Tuesday afternoon, Elizabeth walked into the *Oracle* office and put her backpack on a shelf. John Pfeifer was sorting through some black-and-white photographs for the sports page, and Penny was looking something up in a tattered, well-worn dictionary. Olivia Davidson, the arts editor, was busy typing.

"Hi, all," Elizabeth said. She pulled up a chair next to Penny and leaned forward. "I have an idea for a story," she said eagerly.

Her editor-in-chief sat back and folded her arms. "OK. What is it?"

"I want to do an article about sexual harassment on high school campuses," Elizabeth explained.

Penny's eyebrows shot up, and Olivia paused in her typing to listen in.

"Do you know of a case of sexual harassment?" Olivia asked.

"No, not exactly," Elizabeth said slowly. She couldn't reveal the story of the girl who had called the hotline about a teacher's questionable behavior. Amy had already told Jessica, and Jessica had already told Elizabeth and Todd. The story had gone far enough.

"Well, what do you mean, then?" Penny asked.

"I mean an article describing what it is, and what it means, and what can be done if it happens," Elizabeth said. "It's a subject that nobody talks about, and I think that's a dangerous thing. A lot of girls can get hurt by the silence."

John put down his photographs and nodded emphatically. "I totally agree, for another reason," he said. "There are lots of things that guys don't realize are offensive to girls unless someone tells them. Men and women see things differently, and sometimes you have to tell guys how a girl sees a situation that might be scary to her."

"I understand what you're saying," Olivia agreed. "But I'm sure any teacher who is coming on to a student knows perfectly well what he's doing."

John nodded again. "I know. I'm just saying that there are *other* good reasons for doing the article besides protecting girls."

"What do you think?" Elizabeth asked Penny.

Penny tapped her pencil against her palm. "Hmm. It's not a bad idea."

"I think it's a good idea, if you want to know my opinion," Elizabeth said firmly. "What do you say?"

"I say yes. But you know, this sort of thing has the potential to make a lot of people very nervous," Penny said. "We should run the idea by Mr. Collins."

35

"But—" Elizabeth began.

"Did I hear someone taking my name in vain?" came a cheerful voice from the doorway.

Mr. Collins, English teacher *extraordinaire* and newspaper advisor, walked in with a smile on his handsome face. "What's up?"

Because Elizabeth knew about his own painful experience, she was nervous, and a little embarrassed, about discussing her idea with him.

"Elizabeth has a story idea that I think you should know about," Penny said without preamble.

"OK. Shoot." Mr. Collins pulled out a chair and straddled it.

Elizabeth cleared her throat. She knew that Mr. Collins was a fair person, and he was always very supportive of their plans for *The Oracle*. But she wished she had had a chance to discuss the article further with Penny before having to run it by him. There was no avoiding it now.

"I want to write a story about the issue of sexual harassment," she said.

Elizabeth could see the color drain from Mr. Collins's face.

"What exactly do you mean?" he asked. "Are you saying this is happening at Sweet Valley High?"

"No, not at all," Elizabeth assured him quickly. "I don't mean to do an exposé or anything like that. I just think it's important for people to be able to recognize sexual harassment if they see it, and to know what they can do about it."

Elizabeth felt the tension increase as Mr. Collins sat

36

without speaking. She was sure that a flood of painful memories was engulfing her teacher.

"Elizabeth," he finally said, "I'm sure you can appreciate that my own involvement in this issue makes it very difficult for me—"

"I know," Elizabeth cut in. "Honestly, I do realize that this will stir up a lot of bad memories for you."

"Not that my personal life should have anything to do with the editorial decisions I make," Mr. Collins said. "But I wish you would reconsider. It could lead to all kinds of mistakes. You could start a real witch hunt without meaning to."

Elizabeth shook her head. "That's not the point. It's an important issue, and I don't see why we shouldn't be able to discuss it."

"I just don't think you should stir up trouble where none exists," Mr. Collins countered. "*If* a teacher here at Sweet Valley is guilty of sexual harassment, then something needs to be done. *If* there is a girl who is being harassed, we should get her to go to the proper authorities. It's not our job to raise a lot of groundless suspicions."

"But isn't it our job to give students information that may be important to them?" Penny argued.

"I promise the article will be fair and fully researched," Elizabeth said. "And I don't think you can assume that an informational article about sexual harassment would start a witch hunt. That's like saying an article about anti-Semitism would necessarily lead students to spray-paint swastikas on the wall."

"This is different, Elizabeth, and I think you

37

realize that," Mr. Collins argued. "Careers are at stake. A false accusation could ruin a teacher's whole life. It nearly did mine."

Elizabeth nodded. "I understand what you're saying, honestly," she said. "But if something ever did happen here—or somewhere else—and the student didn't know where to turn for help . . ."

"That would be tragic," Penny said simply.

Mr. Collins ran a hand through his reddish blond hair and sighed. "OK," he said with obvious reluctance. "But I'd like to ask you to clear it with me after the first draft."

Elizabeth was about to object, but Penny cut her off. "That's fair enough," she said. "That's your job as advisor."

"I'm glad you see it that way," he said quietly as he got up to leave.

When he was gone, Elizabeth let her breath out in a rush. "This is going to be harder than I thought," she said.

Four

On Wednesday after school, Ginny took the bus directly to Project Youth. Kathy greeted her and took her into the office for her second hour of counselor training, which covered all the related social services available in the area. Ginny gave her full concentration to the information on substance abuse programs, runaway shelters, and family therapy centers, even though she kept sneaking glances at the clock. When Mike called, *if* he called, she had to be in on the switchboard, not in Kathy's office. But the hour went by quickly, and when Ginny went into the switchboard room, she saw that the lines were quiet.

"Hi," she said shyly when a girl she didn't know smiled. "My name is Ginny."

"I'm Cynthia. I hear you just started," the girl said. "How's it going so far?"

"Fine, I guess," Ginny said. "I get to solo today."

"Great. Oh, a call," Cynthia said as one of the lines lit up. "Hello, Project Youth. What's on your mind?"

Ginny sat down and put on a headset. Her heart was pounding, and she took a deep breath to relax.

"Over to you by special request," Cynthia said to Ginny, pointing to the blinking hold button. "This guy is asking for you specifically."

Ginny's spirits soared. She adjusted her headset and pressed down the button in front of her. "Hello?"

"Ginny, is that you? This is Mike. Remember me?"

"Remember you?" Ginny laughed with relief. *He had really called!*

"Of course I remember," Ginny said quickly. "I'm really glad you called back. How is it going?"

"Well," he began, "at first, I didn't think I would be able to go through with talking to my mother. But then I figured I had nothing to lose."

"Mmm-hmm," Ginny murmured encouragingly.

"So I did. I asked her to go for a walk with me last night after dinner, and I just told her how I felt. I started out by saying that I was glad she'd found someone new to love, but then I said I felt kind of abandoned. She started crying," he said softly.

"What else did you talk about?" Ginny asked.

"Mostly we talked about my dad," Mike said. "We never really did, after he died. And there were some things I wanted to ask my mom about him."

"So you didn't really talk about what's going on right now," Ginny said.

"No. It just seemed . . . at the time, what I really wanted was to talk with my mother and just be honest with her."

"I think that's great," Ginny said. "I bet the rest will come naturally. You just have to give it time."

Mike chuckled. "I know. I always want everything to happen instantly, but some things take a while. If it's worth waiting for, you just have to sit and wait."

"Maybe you should be the one on this end of the line," Ginny teased.

"No way. I could never do what you're doing," Mike said. "You've been fantastic."

"Come on, all I did was sit here and listen. That's what the hotline is for."

"Well, I still say you're terrific," Mike insisted. "It's going to be tough for a while, though, while I'm trying to work things out with my mom and Joe. Is it OK if I call again?"

"Of *course* it is," Ginny said emphatically. "You don't have to ask. Just call whenever you need someone to listen."

"What about if I need *you* to listen?" Mike asked. "Are you there only on Mondays and Wednesdays?"

"That's right." Ginny tucked one foot up

41

underneath her. "I'll be here if you need a friend to talk to. And you know what I think? I think you're going to be fine."

"Well, I hope so," Mike said. "I'm not really wild about taking on Joe."

"Don't look at it as though you're enemies," Ginny suggested. "Have the attitude going into the discussion that you're friends. You have something important in common, you know."

"Like what?"

"Like you both love your mother," Ginny said. "That's a pretty major common denominator."

Mike sighed. "OK. I'll give it a shot and let you know how it turns out."

"And listen, if you need to talk before Monday, just call anyway. All the counselors here are really good listeners, I promise."

"No way," Mike said with a laugh. "You're my one and only."

Ginny was silent for a moment. She knew what Mike meant, that she was his one and only counselor on this problem. But she almost wished those words meant something else—something really special.

"OK," she said finally, trying her best to keep her voice steady. "Call me on Monday, then. I'll be here."

"Great. Thanks again. I'll talk to you on Monday."

When Ginny hung up another button started flashing, and she had to put Mike and his problems out of her mind. It was not until later that evening that she began to relax from the hectic, intense pace of working on the switchboard.

"So, did he call?" Denise asked on the phone after dinner.

"Yes, he did," Ginny replied. She flipped through her Project Youth notebook, reviewing some of her notes from her training sessions. She wondered if there might be a family counseling group that Mike and his folks could join. Wedging the phone between her ear and her shoulder, she underlined the names of two agencies to tell him about.

"Hello? Hellooo-oooo," Denise said. "Wake up, Ginny. You're on the phone, remember?"

Ginny grabbed the receiver with a laugh. "Oh, sorry."

"Aren't you going to tell me any of the details?"

"There's nothing to tell, really," Ginny said. "He called, we talked, the end. And before you ask, no, he didn't declare his undying love for me, OK?"

Denise chuckled. "I wasn't going to ask that."

"Yeah, sure," Ginny said, rolling her eyes. "I'll run this by you one more time. This is telephone counseling, not dial-a-date."

"OK. OK! I got it. It's too bad it's not, though," Denise added.

"Hmm," Ginny mumbled noncommittally. She carefully closed her notebook and placed her hand on it. She didn't want to tell her friend just how much she agreed.

For the rest of the week, Ginny threw herself into her schoolwork, and on Friday night she went to the basketball game with Denise.

"Score, score!" Denise screamed as Jay ran downcourt with the ball.

Jay jumped and slam-dunked the ball, and then turned around and waved to Denise. Ginny felt a small twinge of wistfulness when she saw that brief moment of connection between them.

Someday, she told herself. *Someday I'll have that, too.*

Jessica placed a bowl of potato salad on the picnic table on Saturday evening and looked back at the house. "Where's Liz?" she asked. "Do I have to do all of this myself?"

Her brother, Steven, who was home from college for the weekend, poured himself a glass of iced tea. "Poor Jess," he said, grinning at Sam. "Slaving away all by yourself."

"I'll help," Sam offered.

"You bet you will," Jessica said. She smiled playfully at her boyfriend. "You'll help, or you'll be sorry."

Todd got up from his seat. "I'll go see where Liz is," he said. "I think she's making some phone calls to research her article."

"What's she working on now?" Steven asked.

"Don't ask," Jessica said. "She's gotten all fired up over this one. Writing newspaper stories is about the only thing she ever talks about these days."

"That's true," Todd said, his voice surprisingly serious.

Jessica watched Todd as he went into the house to find Elizabeth. Was it her imagination, or did Todd seem a little bit impatient?

"With all the time Liz puts in on homework

and newspaper articles, I'm surprised she has any time at all for Todd," Jessica said.

"What matters is quality time, not quantity," Sam said, running a finger up her arm in a way that gave her shivers.

A moment later, Elizabeth came outside, hand in hand with Todd. Jessica detached herself from Sam and hurried to her sister. "I have to ask you something," she said, pulling Elizabeth aside.

"What?" Elizabeth asked, watching Todd sit down at the table with Steven and Sam.

Jessica narrowed her eyes. "Let me give you a piece of advice. I'm serious," she added quickly when she saw Elizabeth's skeptical grin.

"OK. What is it?" Elizabeth asked.

"Don't get so wrapped up in this sexual harassment research," Jessica cautioned her.

Elizabeth smiled. "Are you worried about me?"

"I'm not worried about *you*," Jessica said dryly. She nodded her head toward Todd. "Just don't forget about Todd. He looks pretty lonely these days."

"Oh, don't be ridiculous," Elizabeth scoffed.

Jessica shrugged. "OK. But don't say I didn't warn you."

When Monday came around, Ginny could hardly wait to get through her third hour of training. Mike called again as soon as she got to the switchboard, and they continued to talk about how Mike could get along with his stepfamily.

Ginny told him about the group counseling services available at Project Youth, as well as at other agencies, and also told him more about her own experiences after gaining a stepfather. Almost everything Mike said struck a chord in Ginny, and he seemed to feel the same way.

By Wednesday, Ginny was almost dancing with impatience to hear from him. His call came through after she'd been taking calls for two hours.

"Ginny? Hi, it's Mike."

"Hi," she said, leaning back and drawing a deep breath. "How's it going?"

"Last night we had a family conference," Mike said, sounding buoyant and happy. "It was a little rough at first, but Joe and I really got through to each other. He said he's been tough on me because he was afraid I was expecting him to take my father's place, and he thought that if he didn't take a firm line, I wouldn't respect him."

"No kidding?" Ginny said.

"Joe's been as nervous and uncomfortable as I've been," Mike explained. "I never realized that. And my mother was trying to stay out of it because she was afraid to rock the boat."

"Wow. Aren't you glad you talked it all out?" Ginny asked.

"I'll say. Each of us was afraid to take the first step, but now we're all talking and we're even planning a family camping trip in a couple of weeks."

Ginny smiled. "That's great! And just think, it's all because you took that first step and talked to your mother."

"No, it's all because of *you*," Mike said.

46

"No—"

"Yes, you're the one," Mike interrupted. "You know, I didn't tell you this before, but remember the first time I called? I was going to run away."

Ginny's throat swelled with emotion. She couldn't speak.

"I even had a bus ticket," Mike went on quietly. "I called out of desperation. But you were so nice, and you gave me a chance to catch my breath. I'll never forget it."

"I'm just really glad you did call," Ginny said, feeling proud and happy and relieved at the same time. "But you're the one who had to do the hard work."

"Yes, but you know what? All the time I was talking to my mom and Joe, I could hear your voice. You have a great voice, Ginny. It's beautiful."

"Oh, I—" Ginny broke off and glanced shyly around the room. The other counselors were busy talking on the phones.

"I really needed a friend, and you were there," Mike went on. "You're special, Ginny. You're a beautiful person. I know you must be so pretty."

Ginny closed her eyes. If he only knew. To have someone think she was pretty was something she had given up on long ago.

"I'm not," she whispered.

"Yes, you are. I can tell," Mike went on earnestly.

"Well, if you say so." Ginny forced herself to laugh.

"Listen, Ginny," Mike said, sounding shy and uncertain. "Can we meet sometime? I want to thank you in person."

47

A dozen wild thoughts clamored in Ginny's mind: phone counselors weren't supposed to meet the callers; she wanted to meet Mike; she didn't want him to see that she wasn't pretty; she wanted him to go on thinking she was pretty; she didn't know *what* she wanted!

"It's against the rules," she finally managed to say. "We're really not supposed to meet."

"Ginny, come on, we're friends. Friends should be able to meet face to face," Mike pressed. "Please. Just once."

Mike's voice was so warm and sincere that Ginny felt her resolve weakening. She *did* feel that they were friends.

"Come on, what do you say?" Mike asked.

"OK," she whispered. "Just *once.*"

He let out a whoop of triumph. "Great! How about Saturday? Somewhere in Sweet Valley?"

"How about outside Casey's Ice Cream Parlor at three?" Ginny suggested. "It's in the mall. I'll wear a green sweater."

"I'll know you, don't worry," Mike said with a laugh. "I'll just look for the prettiest girl there!"

Ginny's heart sank. "Wait—"

"See you on Saturday. Bye." Mike hung up.

Ginny took off her headset and covered her eyes with her hand. What had she done? As soon as Mike met her he would see what a mistake he'd made. He would be polite, she was sure, but he wouldn't want to see her again. That would be the end of their relationship, such as it was. Knowing that she was going to lose his friendship and admiration was very, very hard, especially when it was so new and wonderful. If only he could just keep calling her on the phone, without ever knowing that she was just plain old mousy Ginny . . .

There has to be a way out of this, she told herself urgently. *And I've got until Saturday to figure it out.*

"Oh, *gym,*" Denise groaned on Friday morning as she and Ginny trooped out to the track with twenty other girls. She eyed the long, seemingly endless oval and suppressed a shudder. "Spare me the fifty-yard dash."

"You'll survive," Ginny said. "Come on, let's stretch out."

Denise sank to the grass and stretched both legs out in front of her; Ginny faced her and did the same. They grabbed each other's wrists and leaned backward and forward, warming up their back and leg muscles. Denise waited for Ginny's usual wry comments about the activities around them. But Ginny seemed preoccupied and tense.

"OK, spill the beans," Denise said, leaning forward over her knees. "What's wrong?"

"Nothing."

"Ha! I don't believe you." Denise narrowed her eyes. "This is me you're talking to."

Ginny frowned and shook her head. "It's nothing, honest. Next topic of conversation, please."

"How's the phone counseling going, then?" Denise asked.

A hot blush spread to the roots of her friend's hair and disappeared, leaving her pale. "Ginny, *what?* Come on, you can tell me."

49

"Oh," Ginny sighed. "I'm in a jam, Denny. Remember that guy I told you about from my first day? Mike?"

Denise brightened. "Yeeeeeeeees?" she drawled.

Ginny looked down at the grass. "He's called a few more times."

"*And?*"

"And he worked it all out with his family," Ginny said with an attempt at lightness.

"And that's what you're so bummed out over?" Denise shook her head. "Come on. It's like I'm pulling teeth here."

Ginny took a deep breath. "And he's really happy, and really grateful, and . . . and he wants to meet me. Tomorrow."

"You're kidding! That's great!" Denise let go of Ginny's wrists and raised two fingers in the air. "She shoots, she scores! I'm so psyched for you."

"De-*nise!* I can't do it," Ginny groaned.

"Oh, Gin, you can, you know you can. Don't be so *shy*. He already likes you. You've already done the hard part."

"But you don't understand," Ginny said, sounding desperate.

"Listen, just be yourself," Denise urged. "You'll be fine."

Ginny shook her head emphatically. "You don't understand," she said again. "He's expecting—listen. It's just a one-time thing. Will you go and pretend to be me?"

"What?" Denise blinked in surprise. She couldn't believe that straight-as-an-arrow Ginny would suggest such a deception. "I can't do that!"

"Sure you can, you know everything about me," Ginny said with a hopeful look in her brown eyes. "He thinks I'm really pretty, and if he meets you, he'll see he's right."

Denise shook her head. "That's crazy! He won't care if you aren't a cover girl."

"Please, Denise. If he meets me, he'll be so disappointed," Ginny said.

"Oh, Ginny," Denise said sadly. "You have to stop being so insecure. You *are* pretty. Believe me."

But Ginny was near tears, and her whole body was rigid with anxiety. "Please, Denise. I just can't do it. It's only this one time. Do it for me. I *never* ask you for anything."

Denise blew the hair out of her eyes with a long sigh. "Oh, OK," she said with a wan smile. "I think it's a mistake, but I'll do it."

Ginny's shoulders sagged, and she closed her eyes in relief. "Thanks. You're the best."

When Elizabeth went to her third class on Friday, her teacher handed her a note from the principal's office. *Mr. Cooper would like to see you during lunch period,* the note read.

Elizabeth slipped the paper into her notebook. The principal often asked her for help in some way; recently she had hosted a delegation of visiting teachers from different countries and had given a speech at the assembly in their honor. She assumed Mr. Cooper had some new project in mind, and forgot about the note until the end of

51

class. Then she hurried down the crowded hallway to the administration office.

"Mr. Cooper's expecting you," one of the secretaries said with a pleasant smile.

Elizabeth nodded, walked to the inner door with the principal's name lettered on the frosted window, and knocked.

"Come in."

"Mr. Cooper? You wanted to see me?" Elizabeth asked as she stepped inside.

"Chrome Dome" Cooper, as he was called by the less respectful members of the student body, waved her toward the desk with an uncomfortable, unconvincing smile. "Elizabeth, yes. Have a seat."

She sat opposite him, smiling politely and waiting to hear what he had on his mind. She noticed a pile of *Oracle* back issues on the corner of his desk. A flicker of uneasiness ran through her.

"Elizabeth, I've been reading over some of your articles for the school paper," Mr. Cooper said, busily straightening some books. "You're going to make an excellent journalist. In fact, you already are an excellent journalist."

"Thank you," Elizabeth said.

"Yes. Yes, the stories you've written for us, and also the articles you've had in the Sweet Valley paper and the *Los Angeles Times* have made us all very proud of your accomplishments."

Elizabeth shifted nervously in her seat. She had a bad feeling about where the conversation was headed.

"You always seem to hit on the issues that matter to our student body," the principal went on.

He tugged at his tie. "I understand from Mr. Collins that you're preparing an article on, er, teacher—er, improprieties. Have you written it yet?"

"I'm still doing research," Elizabeth said carefully. "I want to make sure my story is really well prepared."

"Very wise," Mr. Cooper said. "But I'm afraid I'm going to have to ask you to drop it."

There was a rolling sensation in the pit of Elizabeth's stomach. "May I ask why?" she said calmly.

"I feel that it is in the best interests of our school not to have such a story in our paper," Mr. Cooper said gravely. "Considering the bad publicity we had when Mr. Collins was—er, having his difficulties. I'm very concerned that people might read this story and assume that something of this nature is occurring in our school. We just can't risk a repeat of that sad incident."

"But Mr. Cooper—"

"I'm sorry, Elizabeth. I know that you would do a fine, impartial, and fair story," he said firmly. "But I just can't allow you to do it. And that's final."

Elizabeth stood up. Her knees were weak. "But Mr. Cooper—"

"I'm sorry, Elizabeth," he interrupted.

Angry and confused, Elizabeth turned and walked out the door.

Five

Ginny paced Denise's bedroom on Saturday afternoon. From time to time, she snapped her fingers and tossed a comment toward the open bathroom door. Denise was inside, applying the last-minute details of her makeup in front of a large, well-lighted mirror.

"His stepfather's name is Joe," Ginny said, leaning into the bathroom.

"Right. You told me that," Denise replied. She opened her eyes wide and batted her eyelashes to dry her mascara.

"And don't forget, I've told him that my dad died, too," Ginny said. "So if he wants to talk about that, you know pretty much what happened."

"Mmm-hmm." Denise rummaged around in her well-stocked makeup drawer. Her movements were

54

brisk but unhurried, as though she were getting ready for a tea party with several elderly aunts.

"You don't really mind doing this *too* much, do you?" Ginny asked.

"Of course I don't mind," Denise said. "It'll be easy. I know everything about you."

Ginny tipped her head to one side and gave her friend a wry smile. "Yeah. The amazing adventures of Ginny Belasca."

Denise grinned. "Did you say amazing dentures?"

"Ha ha."

"Anyway," Denise went on breezily, "my alternative was going to another basketball game this afternoon, and to tell you the truth, I can only take so much basketball."

"I'm surprised," Ginny said. "I thought you liked cheering for Jay."

"Rah rah." Denise shrugged. "It gets a little old."

"Oh." Ginny felt slightly embarrassed by Denise's attitude toward Jay but she could not say why. "Does Jay know you're meeting Mike?"

"No way. He'd never understand," Denise said with what sounded to Ginny like sarcasm. "During basketball season he has only one thing on his mind, and if you try to start a conversation about anything else—forget it. Now come on, fill me in on more of the details about Mike. I don't want to goof up."

"OK. They moved from Nevada," Ginny said, thinking back over the conversations she had had with Mike. "He was on the track team at his old school—hurdles and four-man relay."

55

"Got it," Denise said. She smiled at her reflection. "How do I look?"

Ginny felt a strange twisting sensation in her heart as she looked at her friend. The forest-green sweater made Denise's hair look even redder and more lustrous than ever, and brought out the gold glints in her brown eyes. Mike certainly wouldn't be disappointed with the girl he was going to meet. But her friend's appearance only made Ginny more aware that she herself would never have lived up to Mike's expectations.

"You look great," Ginny said quietly.

Denise turned around, folded her arms, and looked at Ginny earnestly. "It's not too late," she said. "You can still go yourself."

"No, no way," Ginny said. "He's been through a lot of rotten stuff lately, and now that he's got his hopes up it wouldn't be fair to disappoint him. He deserves a break."

"To be *saved* from you?" Denise asked with a dumbfounded expression. "Did it ever occur to you that he wants to meet you because he trusts you? This is a pretty big lie to be tricking him with."

Ginny felt her face redden. "It's not a trick," she said quickly, glancing at the clock. "You should get going. It's two-thirty."

Denise sighed. "OK. Suit yourself. Are you sure you don't want to tag along, listen in from behind a newspaper or something?"

"No, thanks." Ginny turned away. She didn't want to see how thrilled Mike would be when he saw how gorgeous "Ginny" was. It would be hard enough thinking about the two of them meeting and having a good time together; she didn't actually want to observe them.

"No, I'll just go home," she continued softly. "Don't forget to tell him it's just a one-time meeting. That I wouldn't feel right continuing to see him, given the circumstances. And call me later and tell me everything, OK?"

"I will," Denise promised. "I still wish you'd go."

Ginny's throat swelled. In spite of the closeness of their friendship, Ginny knew she could never make Denise understand certain things. Denise had never known what it was like to feel awkward and out of place. Ginny knew she could never really make her friend understand why she couldn't go through with meeting Mike herself.

"No, forget it," Ginny said, giving Denise a bright, false smile. "I didn't *really* want to meet him, anyway," she lied. "I only said yes because he was so insistent."

"Well, if you're sure . . ." Denise said.

"Positive. Let's go. You can drop me off at my house on your way." Ginny took Denise's arm and steered her out of the room. Ginny had just one thing on her mind: to get it over with.

As Denise cruised for a parking space outside of the mall, she formulated an elaborate scenario in her head. She would tell Mike the truth from the beginning. She would simply explain that Ginny was so shy that she was embarrassed to meet him. Then she could arrange a surprise meeting between Mike and Ginny, and they would fall in love, and then Denise and Jay and Ginny and Mike could do all kinds of things together. Ginny had said she didn't really want to meet Mike, but that was just how Ginny was—too bashful and insecure for her own good. And it certainly *sounded* as though Mike liked Ginny. He kept calling her at the hotline, after all, even though the crisis was on its way to a peaceful resolution. That could mean only one thing: He liked her. And once he got to know the real Ginny, he'd love her.

The more Denise thought about it, the better she liked her plan. She'd have to find a delicate, reasonable way to explain the switch, and it might take some fancy explaining. But if Mike really was as nice a guy as Ginny said he was, he was bound to understand. She pulled the car into a parking spot and nodded decisively.

"I'll do it," Denise said under her breath as she opened the door. She walked slowly into the mall's food court. Just thinking about playing Cupid put a sparkle in her eyes and a smile on her lips as she stopped outside Casey's.

"Ginny? Is that you?"

Denise turned. Her greeting died on her lips, and her pulse began pounding in her ears.

"I'm Mike Perrine," the boy said with a warm smile. "You're Ginny, aren't you? You're just as pretty as I knew you would be."

For several seconds, Denise couldn't think of a thing to say. Her face felt hot, and she put her palms against her cheeks to hide her blush. She felt as ridiculous and awkward as a thirteen-year-old.

What's happening? she asked herself wildly. *Is this love at first sight?*

The moment she had laid eyes on Mike, all thought of telling him the truth had evaporated like mist in strong sunlight. He was incredibly handsome. His brown hair was combed back from his forehead, and a scattering of freckles crossed his nose. His eyes were brown and he was smiling at her. She felt powerless to do anything but smile back at him.

"Are you OK?" he asked when the silence stretched out.

"Oh, sorry," Denise gasped. "I just—" She laughed and shook her head.

"Do you want to get some ice cream?" Mike asked.

She shook her head again. "No, thanks."

"Would you rather go somewhere else?" he asked her politely. He seemed puzzled.

Denise pulled herself together with an effort. "I don't know why I'm so tongue-tied," she said. She thought quickly. "I'm used to talking to you on the phone. I guess I'm not much good in person."

"You're great in person, Ginny," Mike said. "I'm really glad you agreed to meet me. You've really helped me out, and I have to at *least* buy you an ice cream cone to say thanks. Unless you're one of those girls who never touches anything fattening."

"I don't—" Denise began automatically. Then she remembered that Ginny was very outspoken on the subject of dieting. "I don't object to ice cream at all," she said with a grin.

"Good. Ice cream is too important to ignore," Mike said playfully. "Let's get cones and just walk. Is that OK with you?"

"It's great," Denise said.

Her mind was still spinning as she followed Mike into the ice cream shop. She didn't want to think too carefully about what she was doing. After all, there was Jay to consider. She couldn't go all mushy over a new boy while she had a boyfriend. But, she reminded herself, this was supposed to be just a one-time meeting. Nothing would come of it. It was merely a one-afternoon piece of acting she had to get through.

But it didn't feel like acting. It felt like falling through space. It felt wonderful.

When they each had an ice cream cone, they strolled through the atrium. Denise kept a sharp lookout in case someone who knew her called her by name. Mike talked about his family and how glad he was that they were all communicating at last.

"We talked some more about our camping trip last night," Mike said as they looked into an outdoor-equipment store.

Denise's mind raced. Ginny hadn't clued her in on a camping trip. "How was it?" she asked, licking a stray drip from her cone.

"How was it?" Mike repeated blankly. "We aren't going until next month."

"Oh, I meant, how did it go, the conversation?" Denise wanted to kick herself for such a stupid blunder. "Did you all get along without arguing with one another?"

60

He smiled and seemed to relax. "Well, it still gets a little hairy sometimes, but I just think about what you said. I hang onto that."

He turned and looked at her with such frank, real liking that Denise felt her knees turn to water. She didn't know what this was all leading to, but she didn't want to make any more slip-ups. But wondering what Ginny would say in answer to each of Mike's questions, as well as watching out to be sure she wasn't spotted, was making her nervous.

"Do you mind if we go outside?" Denise asked, glancing around. "It's so crowded in here."

"Sure."

They walked outside and found a bench that faced a landscaped area next to the mall.

"That always makes me feel so sad," Mike said, looking over at a homeless woman who was sitting on another bench with a loaded shopping cart at her side.

"I know what you mean," Denise agreed quickly. "Sweet Valley used to be such a nice place—you never saw that kind of thing."

Mike turned to her, his eyebrows raised in surprise. "What?"

"I mean—" Denise gulped, realizing she had just said something incredibly superficial and insensitive. She didn't even mean it, but had just blurted out the first thing that came to her mind. Ginny would never have said that in a million years. Ginny would have said—

"I mean, Sweet Valley used to be the kind of

place where people like that woman would be taken care of," she said. "It makes me sad that people don't seem to care anymore."

Mike's smile returned once again. "I'll be right back," he said suddenly.

Denise watched as he walked to the other bench and gave the bag lady a few dollars. *He's so nice*, Denise thought. *He's so nice.* She wanted to draw the afternoon out, to delay the moment when they would have to part forever.

"Would you like to go somewhere?" Mike asked when he had rejoined her.

"I don't care—whatever you want," Denise replied vaguely. "It doesn't matter."

They sat in silence for a few moments. Then, suddenly, Mike stood up. "Listen, I'm sorry, maybe this was a bad idea," he said.

Denise stared at him. "What?"

"I get the feeling you aren't very comfortable with me," Mike said.

"No, why do you say that?" Denise asked quickly. "I *do* feel comfortable with you."

"Of course you'd say that," Mike said, smiling apologetically. "You're so nice. But you don't seem the same as you did on the phone. Even your voice sounds different. Face it, I was really pushy about meeting you in person. You didn't want to, but here you are, being polite and putting up with me. I should have realized you agreed only because I was being such a jerk."

"You weren't, you aren't!" Denise said, putting a hand on his arm. She felt a moment of panic. Maybe Mike was too smart and sensitive to be fooled, she thought. All she knew was that she wanted desperately for him to like her and be happy being with her.

"Listen, I'm not sorry at all that I agreed to meet you," Denise said softly.

Mike sat down again, and leaned forward to rest his elbows on his knees. When he turned his head to look at her, his eyes were sad. "Is it that you have a boyfriend? Is that why you didn't want to meet me?"

A hot, nervous flush spread across Denise's face. She had hardly given Jay a second thought from the moment she had met Mike. But there must be a reason for that, she decided. Maybe she and Jay really weren't meant for each other. Lately, it had seemed, all he ever wanted to talk about was basketball, and she couldn't imagine him ever thinking of running back to give money to a homeless woman. Mike was sensitive, intelligent, considerate, and thoughtful. And although Jay was no Neanderthal brute, he certainly didn't have those qualities that Mike obviously had in such abundance.

"I'm having a wonderful time," Denise said, looking straight into Mike's eyes. She *couldn't* tell him the truth now.

Because she knew she wanted to see Mike again. She had promised Ginny to meet him only once. But neither she nor Ginny could have guessed that this would happen, that Denise would fall like a ton of bricks for Mike. It had to be fate that had brought her and Mike together. It had to be.

"A wonderful time," she repeated softly.

"Are you sure?" Mike asked doubtfully.

"Positive. And to prove it, I wish we could see each other again," Denise said.

Mike's face lit up. "You do? Honest?"

"Honest," Denise said. "Why don't we meet at the movie theater on Wednesday? Would that be OK?"

"That would be great," Mike agreed. "You're sure you want to?"

"I'm the one who suggested it, right?" Denise teased. "Let's make it the late afternoon show, though."

"Won't you still be working on the hotline?" Mike asked.

Denise thought quickly. It was so difficult trying to keep in mind that she was supposed to be *Ginny*. "Right, I forgot. Let's make it the seven o'clock show. How's that?"

"Sounds great," Mike said. He took her hand in his and pressed it gently. "Even if you didn't want to meet me today, I'm glad you did. You're just as beautiful and wonderful as I knew you would be."

Denise felt a glow of happiness rush through her, leaving her fingertips tingling. She hadn't felt this way with Jay in a long, long time.

"Thanks," she said shyly. "I'll see you on Wednesday night."

Six

"So?" Ginny asked. "What happened?"

Denise sighed. "He's so wonderful!"

"Really?" Ginny pulled the phone into her lap as she leaned back on the sofa and stared at the ceiling. She hoped she didn't get too depressed listening to Denise's story. "Start from the beginning," she said, gripping the receiver a bit more tightly.

Denise drew a deep breath. "Well, let's see. He spotted me first, and when I turned around, he said something like, 'I knew you'd be pretty.' "

"He was right about you and wrong about me," Ginny said softly. "That's why I suggested doing this."

"But you know what?" Denise said. "He meant that he knew you were a beautiful person. Beautiful on the inside."

"No, he meant beautiful on the outside," Ginny

65

insisted. "So he saw you, and bingo—beautiful girl."

"I don't think he's like that," Denise said. "He's not that kind of a guy."

Ginny rested her cheek against a pillow. She was half inclined to end the conversation before it began to hurt too badly. "OK," she said with a sigh. "Go on. What kind of guy *is* he?"

"He's great. He's so nice, and sensitive, and thoughtful, and all those things that you always wish guys would be, but almost never are. Know what I mean? He actually gave a homeless woman money. Isn't that nice?"

The enthusiasm in Denise's voice was unmistakable. The realization made Ginny feel like crying.

She already has a boyfriend, she told herself sorrowfully. *It's not fair.*

"I really like him a lot," Denise went on. "I guess you can tell."

"Does he like you?" Ginny asked. The moment the words left her mouth, she wished she hadn't spoken.

"I guess so. I'm going to see him again," Denise said.

Ginny closed her eyes and her stomach rolled over.

"Ginny? I won't, if you don't want me to. I mean, he was your friend first," Denise pointed out.

"No, don't be ridiculous," Ginny said, hoping her friend wouldn't hear the quiver of disappointment in her voice. "I'm the one who asked you to meet him. Just because I've talked to him on the phone doesn't give me exclusive rights."

"Are you sure? It's just that . . . I don't know how to explain it," Denise went on, her voice wondering and dreamy. "There was this instant attraction that I've never felt before. I can't believe it's happened. There really is such a thing as love at first sight."

"That's great," Ginny said. "That's really great."

"We're going to the movies together on Wednesday night," Denise went on. "I can hardly wait until—"

"Hey, hang on a second," Ginny cut in. "Aren't you forgetting something—*someone?* What about Jay? Where does he fit in?"

There was a long pause. Ginny waited.

"Well, I don't know," Denise admitted at last. "Jay and I are going to the Beach Disco tonight, but I don't really want to. All he ever talks about these days is the basketball team, rock concerts, whether or not he should get a dirt bike like Michael Harris' . . ."

"You can't have two boyfriends at the same time," Ginny said. "You know that's not right."

"I know," Denise admitted.

"So what are you going to do about it?"

"I'm not sure," Denise said nervously. "I'll figure it out."

"Tonight?" Ginny asked.

"I don't know. Maybe," Denise said. "I have to go," she added quickly. "Bye."

"Bye. And—thanks for—meeting Mike for me," Ginny forced herself to add.

* * *

On Monday afternoon, Ginny sought out Denise in the noisy cafeteria. Her friend was sitting with Jay, and they both looked sullen and moody.

"Hi," Ginny said, pausing uncertainly by their table. "Can I sit with you guys?"

"Sure," Jay replied. He glanced irritably at Denise.

"You could make a little room," Denise told him icily. "You *could* even get her a chair."

Ginny's cheeks burned. "Don't—I'll do it."

"No, *I'll* do it," Jay insisted. He stood up and dragged over an empty chair, and then sat down with a frown.

"What a gentleman," Denise said, tossing back her hair.

Jay threw his hamburger down on his plate and pushed his chair back abruptly. His face was stormy. "OK, that does it," he fumed. He stood up and walked away.

Ginny was frozen with embarrassment. She stood where she was, not wanting to sit, and not knowing if she should leave. Denise continued to eat her salad with an attitude of careful concentration.

"What's going on?" Ginny finally asked.

"He's so immature sometimes," Denise said, looking up. "That's the problem with going out with a guy who's younger. He's like a little kid."

Ginny glanced across the cafeteria to see Jay join a large table of boys. "But he's *always* been like that," she said. "You've always known he was younger than you. Nothing's different."

"Maybe *I'm* different," Denise said. "Could you sit down? I'm getting a stiff neck looking up at you."

Still flustered, Ginny sat down and looked earnestly at Denise. "Does this have anything to do with Mike? It's not fair to start criticizing Jay for things that you never minded before, just because you've met a new guy."

"I know," Denise said. She rested her chin in her hand. "I know it's not fair, and that's why I think I should break up with Jay. I'm really wondering what I ever saw in him."

"Break up with him?" Ginny's heart sank. "Denny, you've only been out with Mike once. Are you sure you want to do this? You and Jay have always had a good relationship."

"Ha," Denise said.

"You have, and you know it," Ginny insisted. "Maybe you just need to communicate with him more. If you don't want to hear about basketball all the time, just say so, but don't break up with him because he's not Mike."

Denise wiped her mouth with a paper napkin. "I know what I'm doing."

"Well . . . OK," Ginny said doubtfully. She opened her carton of milk and felt a fresh wave of confusion wash over her. Originally, the plan had been for Denise to meet Mike once and explain that because of Project Youth's rules and Ginny's own feelings, it could only be a one-time thing. But that simple plan was getting more complicated by the moment. And Ginny had no idea where it was all going to lead.

69

*   *   *

Across the cafeteria, Jessica watched Jay McGuire storm away from Denise Hadley, and raised her eyebrows in a speculative arch. She had tried breaking them up once because she had wanted to date Jay herself. At the moment, she was happily committed to Sam. But she figured it was always good to keep tabs on these things. She filed away the information in her possible-breakups file, and then turned her attention back to her own table.

Her sister and Penny were sitting at the next table, speaking together in low voices, and their expressions were intense.

"Is this a private conversation?" Jessica asked, scooting her chair toward them.

"They're plotting your overthrow as Miss Teen Sweet Valley," Lila said. "Look out."

"Come on, what gives?" Jessica pressed her sister.

"It's nothing—" Elizabeth began.

"It's not nothing," Penny cut in. "I'm taking this very seriously."

"So am I," Elizabeth said.

"OK, now we're all curious," Enid Rollins said with a smile. "What are you two getting so worked up about?"

Lila yawned. "Probably something like whether or not to change the typeface in the newspaper."

"Hardly," Penny said dryly. She looked at the students sitting at both tables. "Listen, if one of

70

you was the victim of sexual harassment, would you know what to do about it?"

"A good kick," Lila muttered.

The others looked uncomfortable. "No," Maria Santelli said. "At least . . ."

"What's this all about?" Winston Egbert asked.

Elizabeth folded her arms. "I want to do a story about sexual harassment—of students, by teachers—but Mr. Cooper thinks it would create some kind of hysterical reaction here."

"Oh, come on," Jessica scoffed.

"It might make some people nervous," Enid said. "The Parent-Teacher Association would probably be pretty upset. They're always concerned with the school's image."

"So what?" Penny demanded hotly. "Newspapers aren't about making people feel good. Newspapers are about information that's important. The question right now isn't whether or not Liz has a good idea for a story, though she does. The question is, will we be told what we can and cannot print in our own paper?"

"Hey," Jessica said. "That's right. Either it's a student newspaper or it isn't a student newspaper. Chrome Dome is telling you to shut up, and if there's one thing *I* can't stand, it's being told to shut up!"

"But doesn't the school administration have a right to some control?" Maria asked. "I mean, we couldn't print articles about something really stupid or disgusting, or articles with an offensive stance."

Todd had been sitting quietly but now he joined the discussion. "But nobody who works on the paper wants to print something stupid or disgusting or offensive. If the editors decide that they have an important story, they should be allowed to run it."

"Right," Enid said. "The school is always telling us to grow up and make hard decisions, but now that Penny and Liz have done just that, the administration is stepping in and saying no, because sexual harassment in the schools is a touchy subject."

Jessica looked around at the group and smiled as an idea occurred to her. "Look," she said confidently, "there's a simple solution to this mess."

"What?" Elizabeth asked.

"Just go ahead with the story," Jessica said.

Winston laughed. "I should have known that would be Jessica's advice. Just do it, and face the music later, that's her *modus operandi*."

"And it works," Jessica said. "Believe me, I do it all the time. You have to make sure you've got a good explanation for when you get caught, but at least you have the satisfaction of having done what you wanted to do."

Penny frowned. "That's not exactly the most responsible attitude, Jessica. Printing the article without the administration's approval could undermine our credibility. Mine and Liz's personally, and also *The Oracle*'s."

"Not necessarily," Todd argued. "If you really believe that this is an important story to run in our paper, then run it. Nobody in this entire school would accuse you of doing it casually."

72

"I don't know, though," Elizabeth said. "It's tempting, but I don't think I'd feel right about going ahead on a story when Mr. Cooper specifically asked me not to. I mean, there wasn't any ambiguity in his attitude."

"It would be a good test," Winston said. "See if the administration would actually gag *The Oracle.*"

"I'd rather try to persuade Mr. Cooper to let me go ahead with the story," Elizabeth insisted. "It would be a lot simpler to get him to see our point of view than to create a huge freedom-of-speech controversy."

"Oh, please," Jessica groaned. "Give us a controversy, Liz. We could use one. I say you should go for it." Jessica patted her sister's hand reassuringly. "Go ahead and write the story, and we'll all watch the fireworks."

By the time Elizabeth arrived at her English class that afternoon, she had developed strong feelings of resentment and disappointment, and they were directed at Mr. Collins. She took her seat without giving him her usual friendly greeting. She nodded coolly when he smiled at her.

Elizabeth guessed that Mr. Collins had discussed the sexual harassment article with the principal. Of course, he had the right—and the obligation—to inform the principal if the paper was planning a controversial story, but Elizabeth couldn't help feeling that he had set off alarm bells prematurely. After all, the story didn't even exist yet. All she had so far was a few pages of notes from her research. Naturally Mr. Cooper would try to axe her article; at this point he couldn't see what kind of an article it was going to be. Hadn't Mr. Collins explained her intentions to Mr. Cooper?

"OK, everyone," Mr. Collins said, closing the door. "Let's talk about *A Tale of Two Cities.* Any comments so far? Anyone absolutely hate this book?"

His candid blue eyes sparkled mischievously. He always started off book discussions by trying to draw out the negative comments, so that the people who were enjoying the book were goaded into arguing.

Nobody answered.

"Elizabeth? How about you? Which of the characters has your attention?" Mr. Collins asked, breaking the silence at last.

Elizabeth raised her eyes, and felt her cheeks flush. She didn't trust herself to speak calmly.

"What's wrong?" Todd whispered.

Mr. Collins turned away. "Anybody? Do I have to carry this whole class on my own?"

There were a few smiles, and after a moment, Maria held up her hand. "I like the character of Lucy Manette," she said.

Elizabeth felt Todd's eyes on her.

She doodled a question mark in the margin of her paper. As the newspaper advisor, and also as mentor for many of his students, Mr. Collins had always stressed that people should stand up for their convictions, that they should take risks to uphold what they believed in.

And Elizabeth believed that it was wrong and

prejudiced of the administration to keep her from doing a story on a difficult and important topic. It was wrong to encourage the newspaper staff— and every other student—to be independent and then to jerk on the leash. It was wrong for Mr. Cooper to decide to stop Elizabeth's story without openly discussing the matter with her—or with Penny.

Elizabeth crossed out the question mark on her notebook with firm, dark strokes of her pen.

I'm going ahead with the article, she thought.

Seven

When Ginny arrived at Project Youth that Monday, Kathy reminded her that she was finished with the training and could get right to work on the switchboard. Barry had praised her work, and Kathy was pleased with Ginny's aptitude in the training sessions.

"You're doing a great job," Kathy said warmly. "Keep it up."

Ginny resisted the temptation to let out a cynical laugh. So far, all she had done on the hotline was to start in motion a ridiculous chain of events. Or not so ridiculous, she reminded herself unhappily as she sat down. Jay was going to pay the price for Ginny's inability to meet Mike.

Keep it up, Kathy had said. Ginny picked up her headset and put it on. She *did* have to keep it up. Now that Mike had met Denise and believed she was Ginny, they would have to continue the cha-

rade, especially since Denise was going to see
Mike again. And if he called while Ginny was at
Project Youth—

"Ugh," Ginny moaned.

"Bad day?" Barry asked from two seats down.

"You have no idea," Ginny replied.

She looked at the switchboard warily. If only
she hadn't been so insanely shy and nervous
about meeting Mike! Now if he *did* call, she would
have to act as though she had spent Saturday afternoon with him. How had Denise acted when
she pretended to be Ginny? The situation was
swiftly going from awkward to impossible. It really would be better if he didn't call, Ginny
decided.

Don't call. Don't call, she prayed silently.

One of the buttons in front of her lit up. She
took a deep breath and pushed it. "Hello, Project
Youth. What's up?"

"Hi, my name is Roy. Can I talk to you?"

"Sure," Ginny said, relaxing into her chair.
"How are you, Roy?"

For the next several minutes, she successfully
put her own problems aside and listened to the
young boy on the other end of the line. He told
her he had been under a great deal of pressure
lately from some friends who were into smashing
mailboxes with baseball bats. He was afraid of getting into trouble, but also afraid of looking like a
wimp in front of his friends. Ginny listened atten-
tively. By the time he was finished speaking, the
boy had admitted that he didn't really like the
others very much. Ginny told him about the free

77

group counseling sessions at the center, and invited him to stop in anytime to talk with other teens about how to deal with peer pressure.

"Thanks," he said. "Maybe I will."

Ginny hung up and glanced at the clock, and the whirl of anxieties came rushing back at her. If Mike stayed true to form, he would call in a few minutes. She fiddled nervously with her hair.

One of the buttons began flashing again. *It's sure to be someone else*, Ginny told herself as she pressed down on the button to take the call.

"Hi, Project Youth. This is Ginny. What's up?"

"The sky." Mike's voice came through loud and clear.

Ginny felt her stomach do a swan dive. There was no way to avoid talking to him now. "Hi, Mike," she said as calmly as she could.

"Listen, I know I shouldn't take up your time when you're on the switchboard," Mike said quickly. "I just had to ask you something."

"Sure, go ahead." Ginny rested her forehead on her hand. This was going to be difficult.

"Are you sure you really want to see me again on Wednesday?" Mike asked. "You seemed—I don't know, a little different on Saturday. Not yourself."

He knows, Ginny realized. If only she could say to him, *Listen, Mike. That wasn't me, that was my friend. I was an idiot and asked her to meet you in my place. But now I wish I'd never done it. Let's clear the slate and start from scratch.*

But she knew how Denise felt about him. And she had to admit that Mike would undoubtedly be very hurt and angry if he found out what she had done. She had to keep up the act.

"No, I was just tired," Ginny lied. "I meant what I said, honest."

"Oh, you were tired. That's it. You know, you even sounded a bit different," Mike said with relief. "But you sound like yourself now."

"Yes, it's me," Ginny said. *If Mike only knew the irony of that statement*, she thought.

"How's it going with your family?" she continued, hoping to steer the conversation onto safer ground.

"Well, like I told you on Saturday, we're going ahead with our camping trip," he answered.

"Right. You told me that," Ginny said faintly. "I remember."

"We're going back to Nevada, to the desert."

"Where you used to live?" Ginny felt her hands shaking.

"Yes. And I talked to my mother and Joe about trying out for the track team," Mike went on. "They realize that it's something that means a lot to me, and that I have the right to continue living my life the way I used to live it. Joe says he'll stop pressuring me to change."

"That's great," Ginny said. "It really is best to be honest about the things that matter the most."

The moment the words left her mouth, it hit her that she had created this entire problem by *not* being honest, and now she had to face the consequences, no matter how depressing and uncomfortable.

"I know. I'm going to try to be honest—totally

honest—from now on," Mike said. "Even those times when I'm afraid to say something because I'm afraid to hurt someone's feelings. Keeping silent just makes things worse."

"That's true," Ginny whispered.

"So listen, I have to be honest with *you*," Mike said seriously. "Don't take this the wrong way, but I had the feeling when we met that you didn't like me. I mean, why would someone as gorgeous as you even be interested in me?"

"That's—that's just dumb," Ginny said, hoping that Mike wouldn't hear the pain in her voice.

Mike sighed. "I know it's dumb, but I wanted to be honest about how I feel."

"Is that why you want to go out with me again?" Ginny asked in a whisper. "Because of how I look?"

"Now that *is* dumb," Mike said with a laugh. "I'll see you on Wednesday. And if you want to wear a paper bag over your head, that's OK with me."

For a moment, Ginny couldn't think of a thing to say.

"Listen, I should go now," she said finally. "Other calls are coming in."

"OK. Bye, Ginny."

Ginny hung up and swallowed the hard lump in her throat. There were two things she knew now that she wished she didn't: Mike had sensed that there was something different about the Ginny he met on Saturday, but because Denise was so attractive he was willing to see her again. She didn't want to believe Mike was so superficial, but she just didn't know what other conclusion to draw.

It was all such a mess. Ginny just didn't want to think about it anymore. All she would get from that was heartache. Things might have been different, but they weren't.

This is how it is, she told herself sternly. *Get used to it.*

Ginny walked with Denise to the cafeteria the next day, trying to get up the nerve to tell her friend about Mike's call, and to suggest the possibility of telling him the truth.

"He called again yesterday," Ginny said finally.

Denise stopped short. "What did he say?"

"He wanted to be sure I—you—still wanted to see him tomorrow night," Ginny said.

"Why wouldn't he be sure?" Denise asked anxiously.

"He said he didn't know why such a pretty girl would want to go out with him."

Denise shook her head. "What did you tell him?"

"I told him yes, you definitely wanted to go out with him," Ginny said.

"Oh, phew!" Denise let out a breathless laugh. "What else did you talk about?"

"Well, it's getting a little tricky, keeping track of what I'm supposed to know," Ginny said a bit tremulously. "But he talked about his family. He's going ahead with the track team tryouts."

"He does look like a runner," Denise said dreamily. "You know, tall and lean."

"Actually, I wouldn't know." Ginny forced a laugh. "Anyway, they're going to Nevada on their camping trip," she said hurriedly.

"Whoa, hold on," Denise said, looking earnestly at Ginny. "Are you bothered by what's happened?"

"No, it's just awkward, that's all," Ginny said, avoiding Denise's eyes.

"If you're sure . . ." Denise said.

Ginny nodded. "Positive. So, like I was saying—camping trip, Nevada."

"That's where he's from, right?" Denise asked, opening the cafeteria door. "This *is* getting confusing. I was kind of flustered, trying to remember everything. Hey, I have an idea."

Ginny paused reluctantly. "What?"

"Why don't you come with me tomorrow?" Denise suggested.

"No way!"

"Yes, think about it," Denise went on. "You can be Denise."

"No, it's too weird," Ginny said firmly.

"Look," Denise said. "If I'm going to be spending time with him, you'll have to meet him sooner or later, right?"

Ginny briefly considered pointing out that they couldn't keep pretending indefinitely, but before she could make that point, Denise continued.

"What do you say?" Denise said. "If you're with me, I won't feel so nervous. That's ironic, isn't it? *You're* usually the one who gets nervous in a situation like this."

"Well . . ." Ginny hesitated. She realized that she *did* want to meet Mike, if only to satisfy her curiosity about what might have been. Seeing Denise and Mike together, seeing that fateful, inevitable attraction that Denise talked about—that might actually be a *good* thing. It would put to rest any lingering hope of Mike's falling in love with *her*.

"Come on, will you?" Denise pleaded. "It's not a pressure situation for you, and you already *know* you two will get along. Please?"

"OK," Ginny said quietly. "I will."

"Great." Denise hugged her enthusiastically. "You're the best, Ginny."

As they faced the crowded cafeteria from the doorway, Ginny and Denise both spotted Jay. He had just left the lunch line with a full tray, and was heading for a group of his friends. Denise's expression hardened.

"Did you break up with him?" Ginny asked.

"Last night," Denise said. "It hasn't been the same between us for a long time. You know I've been complaining about him for a while, right? Face it, the relationship was stale. I just didn't realize *how* stale it was until I met Mike. Listen, I don't want Jay to see me. I'm going to the library, OK?"

"OK." Ginny watched her friend hurry out the door. Then she heard someone call her name. Jay was making his way through the crowd toward her.

"Ginny," he said as he joined her at the door, "what's with Denise?"

"I don't know," Ginny said. It was another lie. She felt that all she had done lately was tell one lie after another.

Jay shook his head glumly. "She broke up with me, you know. Just out of the blue. I can't figure it out."

"I'm sorry," Ginny said. And she was. She had always liked Jay, and she felt that the unhappiness he was feeling was partly her fault.

"Well, I guess there's no use trying to change her mind," Jay said sorrowfully.

"I think she's just going through something right now," Ginny said cautiously. "Just—don't hate her."

"I don't," Jay said, giving her a sad smile. "Who could?"

Ginny shook her head with an ironic smile. "Nobody."

Elizabeth set her tray down on a table and pulled her notebook out of her bag. Glancing up, she noticed Ginny Belasca standing in the doorway of the cafeteria. Elizabeth caught her eye and beckoned her over.

"Hi, Ginny," she said as the other girl sat down at the table with her. "How are you?"

"Oh, fine," Ginny replied.

Elizabeth tapped her notebook with her finger. "Can I ask you something? You're working at Project Youth, right? I wondered if you could answer a few questions," she asked.

"You know I'm not *supposed* to discuss my calls with anyone," Ginny said with a smile.

Elizabeth smiled back. "I did a story about the hotline a while ago, so believe me, I know the rules. Kathy Henry sure made them clear enough. I was just wondering what the counselors are trained to do if a girl calls in to say she's being harassed by one of her teachers. You know, being pressured into a personal relationship."

Ginny frowned thoughtfully. "Well, I haven't been working on the hotline that long, so I don't have any personal experience with that kind of question. But part of my training included studying lists of other kinds of social service agencies. There's a rape crisis center that also handles sexual harassment. I can get the number for you."

"OK, that's good," Elizabeth said as she scribbled in her notebook. "I could call the rape crisis center and ask what kind of advice they'd give in this situation."

"Kathy talked about sexual harassment a little bit," Ginny added. "With adults, the first thing to do is for the woman to ask the man to stop. But when a young girl is involved, she's usually too embarrassed or scared to do that. So we're supposed to suggest talking to a counselor at the rape crisis center. You know, someone who will believe what the girl says, and help her."

Elizabeth nodded and continued jotting notes. "This is good."

"You're doing a newspaper article on sexual harassment in schools?" Ginny asked.

"I'm just at the research stage right now," Elizabeth admitted. "I'd *like* to write an article about it."

"Call Kathy," Ginny suggested, rising. "She knows all the agencies."

"Thanks. I'll do that," Elizabeth said as Ginny walked away.

When she was alone, Elizabeth glanced through her pages of notes. So far, she had only a few scribbled phone numbers and lists of contacts. She had been dragging her feet a bit on writing the article, because she was still not certain that what she was doing was right.

It *was* remotely possible that a student who was troubled or upset about something entirely different might read an article on sexual harassment and misunderstand a teacher's friendliness to her. Elizabeth knew that when she was feeling down, she sometimes misconstrued words or gestures, even from people she knew well. And if a troubled student went so far as making a false accusation, that was the sort of disaster that could never be totally cleared up. Elizabeth knew that even when an accused person was acquitted in court, people still wondered. A lasting taint of suspicion could ruin a teacher's career, just as it had nearly ruined Mr. Collins's.

But it was also true that if a vulnerable, frightened girl was being harassed for real, and didn't know where to turn for help, that could ruin much more than a career. That could ruin the rest of a girl's life.

Elizabeth met with Penny later that afternoon to talk about her own confusion over what to do.

"I agree that both sides are valid," Penny said. "But that's sort of beside the point right now. The bigger question that I'm worried about is this: are there subjects that the administration can say are off limits? Are we really journalists, or is this some kind of game we're playing?"

Elizabeth shook her head. "I know. I know that's an important issue. But all I wanted to do was write a story on a subject I think needs discussing."

"Exactly," Penny said with a militant flash in her eyes. "In our judgment, as editors of this paper, this is an article that needs to be written, and I think we should be allowed to use our own best judgment in deciding how to write and present it."

"You're right," Elizabeth agreed.

"It's up to you, Liz," Penny said seriously. "It's your story. Do you want to write it?"

"Yes," Elizabeth said. "I do."

"OK. That's our decision," Penny said as she folded her arms.

Elizabeth smiled. "Thanks. I appreciate your backing me up like this."

"So you'll go ahead and write the story?" Penny asked.

"Yes." Elizabeth met Penny's eyes. "I just hope it doesn't all blow up in our faces."

Eight

"We have to think of a good reason for your being here with me," Denise said as she parked the car behind the movie theater on Wednesday evening. She checked her reflection in the rearview mirror and added, "You know, why I brought you along on a date."

Ginny shrugged. "Say anything you want," she said carelessly. "Say I'm depressed and you wanted to cheer me up."

"If that's what you want," Denise said with a grin. She was full of nervous energy, and looked three times in her purse for the car keys after she had locked the car door.

"Now, remember," Denise said. "You're Denise, I'm Ginny. Don't forget and call me Ginny."

"This is so weird," Ginny said. "Why did I agree to this?"

Denise swooped down on her to give her a hug. "Because I asked you to and you're so nice."

"Oh, that's right." Ginny shook her head. It seemed as though all she had done lately was agree to things her better judgment had warned her against. She never should have agreed to meet Mike in the first place, never should have asked Denise to meet him in her place, never should have agreed to meet Mike now and pretend to be Denise. It was insane.

"Now, come on," Denise said, tucking her arm into Ginny's. "He might be here already. I can't wait for you to meet him."

"I can't wait, either. But Denise?" Ginny asked, pausing for a moment. "What if he recognizes my voice?"

Denise waved her hand dismissively. "He won't. He thinks I'm Ginny. It wouldn't be human nature for him to wonder suddenly if we'd switched identities."

"I guess you're right," Ginny said.

When they rounded the corner and came to the front of the theater, Denise grabbed Ginny's wrist tightly. "There he is! Isn't he adorable?"

There was a crowd outside the theater, but Ginny knew Mike right away. She would have known him anywhere. That was Mike, her friend Mike. No—*Denise's* friend Mike.

It won't be hard at all to pretend I'm depressed, Ginny told herself.

"Hi, Mike," Denise said, her eyes glowing with happiness as they joined him.

"Ginny, hi," Mike said to Denise. Then he glanced at Ginny. "Hi."

Denise put her hand on Ginny's shoulder. "This is Denise," she said. "Do you mind that she came along?"

"No, of course not," Mike said. "How are you?"

"Fine," Ginny answered in a low voice.

"Did we ever meet somewhere before?" Mike asked.

"No, I doubt it," Ginny said quickly.

"You didn't by any chance ever live in Nevada, did you?" Mike went on.

Ginny shook her head. "Well, maybe in a past life," she suggested with a weak smile. "But with my luck, if I'd lived in Nevada, I was probably an armadillo."

Mike laughed. "Hey, I think I've met some of your cousins, then. Do they like garbage?"

"They love it," Ginny said brightly. *Mike is just as nice in person as Denise said he was*, she thought.

"I knew you two would hit it off," Denise said brightly.

"Ginny told me you go to Big Mesa," Ginny said. "How do you like it?"

"I just moved there, but I think it'll be OK. I went to the track and field tryouts today," he said.

"Oh! That's great!" Ginny cried.

Mike grinned. "Wow. Thanks for your support."

"Come on, let's go in," Denise said.

Ginny looked at her friend. She had almost for-

90

gotten that Denise was there with them. "Right," she mumbled.

While they stood on line for tickets, Ginny couldn't help but notice that the flow of conversation between Denise and Mike wasn't nearly as easy and comfortable as it was between Mike and herself. Several times, some quick retort that she knew Mike would appreciate was on the tip of her tongue, but each time, she bit it back.

I'm not here to butt in, she reminded herself. *I shouldn't even be here at all.*

Inside, Denise sat between Ginny and Mike. Ginny was glad she wasn't sitting next to him herself. It would have been too tempting to keep up a running commentary with him about the film, which was truly terrible.

"Let's go somewhere for ice cream," Mike suggested when they were making their way back up the crowded aisle at the end of the show. "What about that place called the Dairi Burger?"

Ginny and Denise exchanged an anxious look. The Dairi Burger was always filled to capacity with Sweet Valley High students. And that made it definitely off limits. There was too much of a chance that someone would call them by their correct names and blow their cover. No, they couldn't risk the Dairi Burger.

"Ginny?" Mike asked.

"Yes?" both girls answered at once. Mike's eyes registered a moment of confusion, and Ginny blushed and looked away.

"Her nickname used to be Denny," Denise explained smoothly.

91

"That's right, I thought you said Denny." Ginny gave Mike a weak smile.

"Let's go to the Lucky Duck," Denise said. "I haven't been there for ages."

Ginny raised a hand to her face so Mike wouldn't see her smile. Mike would think it was very peculiar for them to choose a place where the waiters were dressed as ducks. At least it wasn't likely they would run into anyone over the age of nine.

"I've never been there," Mike said.

"You're in for quite an experience," Ginny said. "It'll quack you up."

"It'll be fun," Denise promised while Mike laughed. "Let's go."

A few minutes later, the three of them were shown to a table in the corner of the brightly painted ice cream shop. Because it was after nine on a school night, the place was almost deserted.

"What can I get you?" their duck waiter asked in a tired voice.

"A little cornmeal and some algae," Ginny said.

Mike let out a hoot of laughter. "I'll have that, too. Unless you have duck soup."

"What?" Denise asked, a bright, puzzled smile on her face.

The duck just looked bored. "What can I get you?"

Denise looked down at the placemat-menu. "Can I have a diet cola—"

Ginny kicked her under the table. "Ginny" wasn't worried about such things as maintaining a model-slim figure, and Mike knew it.

"I mean, chocolate ice cream with marshmallow topping," Denise corrected herself.

"I'll have maple walnut," Ginny said.

"Hey, that's my favorite," Mike put in. "I'll have that, too."

Denise rested her chin on her hand. "I'm glad you two get along so well."

Mike smiled at Ginny. "Me, too."

Denise excused herself and went to the ladies' room. She felt as though she were walking on air, and she knew that the Lucky Duck would always seem like a magical place to her, even with its silly decorations and ridiculous duck waiters. Maybe she and Mike would make it their own special place, she mused as she checked her makeup in the mirror. She carefully flicked a tiny clump of mascara off her lashes, smiled at her reflection, and turned back to the door.

She paused when she caught sight of Ginny and Mike. They were laughing together. A smile crossed Denise's face. It was a relief to see Ginny so relaxed and comfortable with Mike. She had been worried that Ginny would be embarrassed and tense with him. But her friend was being her usual witty self, the self that very few people ever got to see.

If only some other guy could see her this way, Denise thought, *he would fall for her in a minute.*

A momentary flicker of doubt surfaced in Denise's mind as she watched Ginny and Mike talk animatedly. When Denise was with Mike, she sometimes felt a strange awkwardness that Ginny very obviously *didn't* feel. *Oh well*, she thought. *It's just that love is making me nervous!*

Just as she sat back down at the table, both Mike and Ginny burst out laughing.

"What's so funny?" Denise asked.

"Oh, hi, Ginny," Mike said. "You're back."

"Did you think I'd gone home or something?" Denise asked, her eyes lingering on his face.

He grinned and shook his head. "No, of course not."

Ginny jabbed at her ice cream.

"So, what were you guys talking about?" Denise asked, hoping to cajole her friend into the conversation.

"Nothing," Ginny said.

"Denise was telling me about the Miss Teen Sweet Valley pageant," Mike explained. "It sounds pretty funny."

Denise shrugged. She could understand the pressure that people put on attractive girls. Being pretty was a very difficult responsibility.

But because she was "Ginny" tonight, she couldn't voice her own real opinions. "Stupid contests, right?" Denise said wryly.

"Still, if you had entered it, I bet you would have won hands down," Mike said. Denise felt her heart flip-flop inside her.

Ginny's spoon clattered into her dish. "I hate to say this," she said, "but it's getting kind of late."

"Sure, we should go," Mike agreed, getting up abruptly.

"I'll be right back." Ginny stood up, too, and headed for the ladies' room.

"Mike, listen," Denise said, following him to the cash register. "I want to tell you something."

He smiled. "Sure. What is it?"

"Well, it's just that . . . when we met you asked me if I had a boyfriend," Denise began. She twisted her hands together nervously. "The fact is, at that time I did. But after I met you, I realized that the relationship wasn't going anywhere."

Mike cleared his throat. "What do you mean?"

"I mean, I broke up with him," Denise confessed. "Because of you."

"But you shouldn't have—" Mike's face flooded with color.

"I'm glad I did," she said softly.

Someone came to the cash register, and Mike turned to hand over their bill. Denise wanted to reach out and brush the hair from his forehead. She thought he was incredibly sweet. She also wondered when he would kiss her for the first time.

"Ginny," he said, "why—I mean, we only—"

"I had to be honest," Denise insisted firmly. "Don't worry about it. I have a good feeling about us."

Mike nodded, and his throat worked as he tried to swallow.

He's so cute! Denise thought. *That shyness is adorable!*

"Let's have lunch together on Saturday," she pressed as Ginny rejoined them.

Mike glanced at Ginny, and then gave Denise a swift smile. "Sure. OK."

"At the Box Tree Café?" Denise stood on tiptoe to whisper in his ear. She didn't want to embarrass him, if it was difficult for him to talk about such things in front of a third person. "It's very romantic."

Mike nodded.

"I'll see you there at twelve-thirty," Denise said. "Bye."

"It was nice to meet you, Mike," Ginny said quietly.

"Yes. Definitely, Denise," Mike said.

After saying goodbye to Mike in the parking lot, Denise tucked Ginny's arm into her own and steered her to her car. "Isn't he just the most adorable guy in the world?"

"Yes," Ginny said softly. "I guess he is."

Nine

Elizabeth arrived at school on Thursday with plenty of time to spare before homeroom. After a quick stop by Mr. Collins's empty classroom, she hurried to the *Oracle* office. A strange, lightheaded sense of detachment came over her. She knew that what she was holding had the potential to cause an enormous commotion at Sweet Valley High. Freedom-of-speech debates between administrations and school papers had caused havoc at other schools, and it could happen at theirs.

Elizabeth opened the door and saw both Penny and Olivia hard at work. "Here it is. The first draft. I already dropped off a copy for Mr. Collins."

Penny slid her pencil behind her ear and held out her hand. "OK. Let's have it."

Elizabeth pulled out three folded sheets of

paper and passed them to her editor. Her article, "When We Are Afraid to Speak," compared censorship to the pressure society put on women and girls not to "make a fuss." Her research on the subject had made one thing clear: girls were usually told by friends and relatives not to report incidents of sexual harassment. It could only lead to embarrassment. All too often, girls were afraid they would be accused of leading the man on. Sadly, that fear often arose from hints dropped by people in authority. The consequences were often tragic: girls were scared silent.

In Elizabeth's view, the pressure being put on her not to write about the subject was very similar. The principal was afraid it would open a Pandora's box of suspicions, and felt it was best just to let the matter alone. The administration was capable of using exactly the same intimidation techniques to keep Elizabeth quiet that a harasser might use to keep a girl from turning him in. She knew Mr. Cooper was concerned about the school's reputation. But freedom of speech carried certain responsibilities, her article argued, such as bringing out into the open the subjects that everyone wanted to sweep under the carpet.

Her article was only partly about teachers coming on to students. Elizabeth had been careful to include other examples of power-play tricks that a teacher might abuse, and to give information on where to go for help. But the main thrust of the article was the point that when we are afraid to speak, our rights and privileges wither away.

"Wow," Penny said when she and Olivia had

finished reading. She whistled and tossed the article onto the table. "This is fabulous, Liz. It's one of the best things you've ever done."

"You think so?" Elizabeth asked, nervously fingering a button on her blouse.

"Definitely," Penny said. "But I'm also positive they'll never let us print it."

Olivia grimaced. "That's for sure."

Elizabeth pulled out a chair. "Can't we print it anyway? Just put it in. How can they stop us if they don't know?"

"I've got some news for you. I got a note from Mr. Cooper's office. They're going to check the galleys for the next couple of weeks," Penny informed her tersely.

A strange prickling sensation crawled up Elizabeth's back. "I feel as if we're being watched."

"I know." Penny shook her head slowly. "If I wanted to be really paranoid, I'd say we shouldn't talk in here, because the office may be bugged."

"Oh, come on!" Elizabeth laughed. "That *is* paranoid! Still, that's just what the article is about," she went on.

Olivia shook her head slowly. "It's like—"

"Totalitarianism?" Penny supplied sarcastically. "Funny, but that's the word that springs to mind. I know the school has a right and a responsibility to make sure we don't print anything inflammatory. But Liz, your article presents a serious, reasonable, and sound argument."

"So what do we do?" Elizabeth asked.

"I'm thinking." Penny ran a hand through her short hair. "I'm thinking."

Just then, the door opened, and Mr. Collins walked into the newspaper office. He was holding a copy of Elizabeth's article, which she had slipped under his door, and his expression was grim.

Elizabeth held her breath. She knew that she wouldn't be able to feel the same way about her mentor if he didn't take her side now.

"What do you think?" Penny asked him.

Mr. Collins smiled at Elizabeth, and in that moment, she knew he would back her.

"This is excellent, Elizabeth, really," he began, taking a seat. "If I had to grade it, I'd have to make up a new grade, one above A-plus."

"Thanks," Elizabeth said.

From out in the hall, she could hear the sounds of students shouting and laughing and slamming locker doors. It all seemed very remote and separate from the discussion going on inside the newspaper office. Elizabeth realized sadly that it wasn't possible to do an article about one discrete thing. Nothing in a school existed in isolation; whenever one string was tugged, it turned out to be attached to a whole web of interconnected questions. Elizabeth's tugs on one string were threatening to pull many things out of line.

"But can we print it?" Penny insisted stubbornly.

"I've told you how I feel about the subject," Mr. Collins said. "I've been a victim myself, but I've been exonerated. I do believe in justice, and I do believe that if you're innocent, people will know it, that ultimately the truth will come out."

"So you're not worried about starting a witch hunt?" Elizabeth asked.

"I won't say I'm not worried about it," Mr. Collins said. "For example, in the news business, there's always a chance that when you print a story about some particularly nasty new crime, some sick person will think it's a great idea and just have to try it himself. But you can't let the fear of copycat criminals stop you from reporting the news. There *is* a certain similarity between that chance and what Mr. Cooper fears may happen. Not so much that a false accusation would be made consciously or maliciously, although I think he is worried about that, too, but that one would be made all the same."

"Isn't he also afraid of bad public reactions?" Olivia asked. "Isn't he afraid some parents might think that where there's smoke, there's fire?"

"Yes, I'm afraid so," Mr. Collins agreed. "But democracy depends on a free press and an informed public. We can't be held accountable for what someone does or thinks after reading the information we print."

"As long as we've presented the information fairly and responsibly," Penny added. "And I think we all agree that Liz has done that."

Mr. Collins nodded. "Granted. However, there is an inflammatory element here, Elizabeth. Your discussion of censorship is going to make a lot of people very angry—Mr. Cooper, the school board, the superintendent, and so on."

"I realize that," Elizabeth said firmly. "But I'm only reporting what's happened."

"Right. But listen. You had better be one hundred and fifty percent sure about doing this," he went on seriously. "Because if we go ahead and print this article, there *will* be trouble."

Elizabeth studied his face for a moment, and a new, alarming thought surfaced. "Will *you* get into trouble for approving the article?" she asked.

Mr. Collins shook his head. "I don't know. Maybe. But I've asked you to be serious journalists, and if you're willing to take the heat, the least I can do is share that heat with you. Maybe I shouldn't have told Mr. Cooper about your intentions when I did. I think now I should have waited to see your finished article."

"Thanks," Elizabeth said. "That means a lot to me."

"Mr. Collins, you're the best," Penny said.

"Just remember one thing," Mr. Collins advised them as the homeroom bell rang. "Be prepared to defend yourselves. Some people are going to have some pretty tough questions for you."

Ginny stood at her open locker, pulling out the books she would need for her next two classes and collecting her thoughts at the same time. It struck her as ridiculous that she could talk so easily to Mike, or to other boys, under certain circumstances, but that she was such a total clam under others.

It's time to start changing that, she told herself sternly.

"Ginny, hi, I'm glad I found you," a voice behind her said.

Ginny turned to see Amy Sutton. "Hi," she said a bit uncomfortably.

"Ginny, can you do me a huge favor?" Amy asked. "I forgot that I have a dentist's appointment this afternoon, and I'm afraid I won't be able to get to Project Youth for my hotline shift. Could you cover for me?"

"Sure. No problem," Ginny said.

"You're a pal. Thanks." Amy waved and ran off down the hall.

You're a pal. Amy's words echoed in Ginny's head.

There had been nothing painful or difficult about their conversation, she realized. There was absolutely no reason to become tense and nervous every time a popular, outgoing person spoke to her. She had to get used to the fact that it was all in her head. Nobody actually treated her like a second-class citizen. It was only her own groundless fears that had kept her apart from almost everyone besides Denise for so long.

By the time the school day was over and Ginny had arrived at Project Youth, she had determined to start changing her life that very afternoon.

She opened the door to the switchboard room, and the three phone counselors who were already there turned to see who had come. For a moment, Ginny felt a wave of anxiety. They were expecting

Amy, and maybe they'd be disappointed to see it was Ginny.

"Hi," she said, forcing herself to sound cheerful.

They smiled. "Hi," Barry said.

"Amy had a dentist's appointment," Ginny began to explain. "I'm sorry—"

"Why?" Barry asked. "You're doing her a big favor by filling in for her. She told me she had asked you, and I know she really appreciates your coming through."

"Oh, well, that's OK," Ginny replied with a shy smile.

I can change, she told herself as she put on a headset. *I can start opening up to people and taking risks.*

"What are you so happy about?" Barry asked her.

Ginny blushed. "Why, was I smiling like a fool?"

"Ear to ear," Barry teased. "And nodding your head, too."

Laughing, Ginny sat back in her chair and waited for a call to come in. *Who can tell?* she thought. *Maybe I can even untangle the knots in the Mike-Denise-Ginny mixup! Maybe Denise will realize Mike isn't the boy for her, and Mike and I can start from scratch.*

Because if there was one thing that kept resurfacing in her mind, it was the memory of the fun she had had with Mike the night before.

One of the buttons on the switchboard began to flash. She reached forward and pressed it down. "Hi, Project Youth."

"Hi," a girl said. "I have this problem that I feel kind of stupid talking to my friends about."

"You can say anything you want here," Ginny offered. "I promise to listen with an open mind."

"Well, my name is Shelley, and my problem—well, it's not really a problem. It's more like just the way it is."

Ginny frowned. "Can you be more specific? I'm not really following you."

Shelley sighed. "I'm tall. Really tall. I know that's not supposed to be a problem, but you know. Lots of people think tall girls look so out of place."

With a start, Ginny realized she knew who Shelley was. Shelley Novak was a junior at Sweet Valley High, and had created something of a controversy when she had tried out for the varsity boys' basketball team. Because she had gone to many basketball games with Denise to watch Jay, Ginny could exactly picture the girl at the other end of the line.

But Shelley had turned her height to her advantage, Ginny knew that. And Shelley had a really nice boyfriend, too. Jim Roberts had helped Shelley to realize her own beauty when he had taken an award-winning photograph of her on the basketball court. Ginny was puzzled by Shelley's confession that standing out in a crowd was a problem for her.

"Well, what exactly is bothering you?" she asked.

"I just can't help feeling unattractive sometimes," Shelley said. "I'm such a beanpole."

Ginny sighed. She knew what it was like to feel that you weren't pretty. But Shelley needed her spirits boosted, not proof that there were other girls who felt just as left out. That knowledge wasn't going to be much comfort.

"And sometimes," Shelley continued, "my boyfriend says things like—oh, I don't know. I feel like he's comparing me to other girls and wishing I were shorter. I guess I'm not very secure about this relationship."

"All I can tell you is that it's normal to feel you don't fit in," Ginny said, remembering how Kathy had once said that most teenagers felt isolated at some time. "Lots of people feel like outsiders for some reason or another. But you know, your boyfriend probably likes you for *who you are*, not just for how you look. Otherwise, why would he be going out with you?"

"That's true." Shelley let out a shaky laugh. "To tell you the truth, I guess I can't get used to having a boyfriend. Sometimes I wake up at night and think I've just been imagining the whole thing."

"Hang in there," Ginny said warmly. "Try to concentrate on being yourself, and on accentuating the things about yourself that you think really *are* attractive."

"I suppose so." Shelley paused, as though thinking. Then she sighed. "Thanks for listening."

"That's what we're here for," Ginny told her. "Call back anytime."

"I will. Thanks."

When Ginny hung up the phone, she looked over at the ghostly image of herself reflected in the window. Ginny knew that she should take her own advice. So what if she wasn't as pretty as Denise was? It wasn't as though she was repulsive! She should concentrate on the things about herself that *were* attractive, just as she had suggested Shelley do. If she went around *feeling* like a drab nothing, that was the image she would project. But if she tried to overcome her insecurities, maybe things would brighten up.

Although it might be too late with Mike, it wasn't too late for someone else, she reasoned. She leaned forward as another line began to flash.

"Hi, Project Youth."

"Hi, my name is Mike. I need to talk."

Ginny froze. She couldn't talk to him yet! She just couldn't. She looked around for someone else to take his call. She couldn't keep pretending to be two people at once, not now. She was still too busy trying to be the real Ginny.

But everyone else was occupied with a call. She had to talk to Mike herself and get through the conversation—somehow.

Ten

"Can I run something by you?" Mike asked. "I'm in a weird kind of jam."

Thinking furiously, Ginny pulled the microphone of the headset a bit farther from her mouth. She lowered her voice a few notches to disguise it.

"Sure, go ahead," she said in a slightly strangled tone.

"I met this girl—well, not exactly met, at first. I can't really explain how," he said. "It was sort of a—a—pen-pal type of situation."

He's trying to protect me, Ginny realized. *He doesn't want to tell this "new" phone counselor that he met me over the same phone line he's using now.* It made her heart ache. And if he was going to go on to say that he was in love with Ginny, meaning Denise, she thought she would just crumble.

"Go on," she said faintly.

108

"Well, we have this great relationship. When I talk to her on the phone, she's funny and smart and incredibly nice. She's wonderful."

A hard lump filled Ginny's throat. She couldn't have spoken a word if her life depended on it.

"But then when I finally met her, it was different. It's really hard to explain, but it's like she's a different person."

"Mmm-hmm," Ginny mumbled. Her mind was spinning. Of course he knew something was different. He would have to be an idiot not to realize that Denise wasn't the same girl he had spoken to so many times.

"The hard part is that once we went out I didn't really like her as much as I thought I would. I mean, she's incredibly gorgeous and all that, just like I knew she would be. But I didn't have a very good time with her. And the thing is, it was *my* idea in the first place to meet her. She didn't want to, but I sort of forced her into it. Now I feel like the worst kind of pig."

Poor Denise, Ginny thought miserably. *She'll be devastated.*

"You shouldn't feel guilty," Ginny managed to say. "Sometimes these things just don't work out the way you expect them to. You can't help that."

"I know." Mike sighed. "She was really wonderful to me before I met her, and she helped me get through some really hard stuff in my life. I feel like I owe her something."

Ginny pressed her hand against her forehead. She was so confused that she could hardly think.

109

The only thing that kept spinning around her head were the words "bitter irony."

"And then, what's even worse is that she broke up with her boyfriend over me," Mike exclaimed. "I feel terrible about it. I don't know what to do."

There was a long pause.

I've made a complete mess out of everything, Ginny thought miserably. *I shouldn't even be here. I'm a total failure at my own life.*

The silence stretched uncomfortably. Then, with an effort, she drew herself together.

"Maybe you just have to tell her the truth," she said, knowing she was a complete hypocrite and hating herself for it. "That's the only way."

"That's what she told me," Mike said sadly. "When she was helping me sort out my problems back when we first got to know each other."

Ginny blinked back tears. "Did it work?" she finally asked.

"Yes." Mike sighed again. "It was hard, but it made everything work out right. In a way, she sort of saved my life. How can I turn my back on her now?"

"I don't know," Ginny said truthfully. "I don't really know what to say."

"Yeah." Mike drew a deep breath. "But wait until you hear the next part. It gets even more complicated."

"Go on," Ginny said softly.

"I met this other girl," Mike said.

Everything in Ginny's sight suddenly blurred and she had to close her eyes. This conversation was rapidly becoming unbearably painful for

Ginny. She hoped she wouldn't have to listen to too many details about Mike's newest love interest.

"She's pretty—not the way the first girl is, but there's something about her. Her beauty is not something you notice at first. I guess it comes out as you talk to her. She's funny, and smart, and really fun to be with. She's everything I was hoping the first girl would be," Mike went on enthusiastically.

It's too late—too late—too late, echoed in Ginny's head.

"Mmm-hmm," she mumbled, trying not to cry.

"I'm just going nuts," Mike went on. "This new girl I met—I think we'd really have a chance if I were free. But I owe the first girl something, don't I?"

"I think so," Ginny whispered. She had to pull herself together. If she let herself go, she would either confess everything to Mike or hang up on him. The first option would only mean humiliation, and the second was a tremendous cop-out.

"I think it's time to be fair to the first girl," she said, fighting for control. "If you don't feel anything for her except obligation, that isn't much of a relationship, you know?"

"I know. That's true, but it doesn't *seem* very fair."

"It isn't fair to let her think your feelings are different," Ginny warned. "I mean, it's going to be hard no matter when you tell her, so it might be best to do it sooner instead of later."

111

Mike groaned. "I know. But I feel like such a jerk. This is all my fault."

Ginny's heart skipped. Mike was one of a kind. Not many people would be so willing to accept the responsibility for such a problem.

"No, I'm sure it isn't your fault," she said. "You can't go on blaming yourself because you don't like the first girl as much as you thought you would. The fact that you're even calling the hotline proves that you're trying to do the right thing."

"Maybe. But I still feel terrible about the whole thing. I know I have to break up with her, and I want someone to do it for me or to talk me out of it—but that's just my own weakness. I know nobody can do it for me."

I'm sorry, Denise, Ginny told her friend silently.

"I guess you know what to do," she said to Mike.

"Yeah." Mike took a deep breath. "Hey, thanks a lot. I didn't mean to lay all this stupid stuff on you."

"That's what we're here for," Ginny said, but her voice rang hollow in her own ears.

"Well, thanks. Bye."

There was a click, and the dial tone began buzzing in Ginny's headset. She sat perfectly still while the tone went on and on and on.

That is the most final sound in the world, she thought vacantly. *A dead line.*

"Goodbye," she whispered.

Jessica struggled into the tight sweater of her cheerleading uniform in the girls' locker room that night. She could hear the swelling roar of voices from outside in the gym as people began arriving for the basketball game. Amy rummaged around in her hot pink duffel bag for her sneakers.

"Ay ouf fees eerd," Amy mumbled. She touched her lower lip gingerly. "Ugh."

"Novocaine?" Jessica asked. "Don't you hate that? Who'd you get to sub for you at the hotline?"

"Inny," Amy said, grimacing.

Jessica examined her sneakers with a critical eye. They were looking very worn and shabby to her. "Isn't it weird how Ginny and Denise are friends? You wouldn't think so. I wonder if Denise will be at the game tonight. You know, she broke up with Jay."

"Dumped him like a ton of old socks, is what I heard," Maria put in. "And now he's free. I wonder if he's going to start dating someone else?"

Amy and Maria gave Jessica arch smiles, but Jessica held up her hands dismissively. "I might have liked him once, but Sam and I are deeply in love." She pointed to her feet. "What's most important to me at the moment is the issue of these crummy sneakers. I can't believe sneakers aren't considered part of the cheerleading uniform. That means I have to buy new ones myself."

Jean West sat down between Jessica and Amy and carefully folded down the cuffs of her socks. She nodded silently across the locker room, where Shelley Novak was putting on her basketball uniform.

"Ut?" Amy mumbled.

"She could go out with Jay," Jean said with a wink. "Teammates have that special bond, you know?"

"She's got a boyfriend," Jessica reminded her. "And there aren't many guys willing to 'look up'," she added with a giggle.

"Oh, come on," Maria said. "Don't be mean. Besides, you never know—Jay and Denise could get back together. It could be just a temporary breakup."

"Uh-uh. I think she has some mystery boyfriend from another school," Annie Whitman put in. "I had to stop my car in the parking lot of the Lucky Duck the other night because there was some weird noise coming from the engine, and I saw Denise and Ginny with this really cute guy in there."

"How do you know he was with Denise?" Jean asked.

Jessica rolled her eyes. "He wouldn't have been with *Ginny*. Come on, let's get out there. There's a whole gym full of people who are just dying to see us."

"That's what they're here for, after all," Annie said, laughing. "The basketball game is just an excuse."

Jessica bent over to give the laces of her old sneakers one last tug. She was in a sour mood over the condition of her bank balance. Recently, Jessica and Elizabeth had appeared on Jessica's favorite soap opera, *The Young and the Beautiful*, and they had been paid quite well for only a week's work. The twins agreed to contribute half their earnings to help pay for their new Jeep. Elizabeth bought a new word processor with her share of what was left. But after Jessica repaid her parents for all the clothes she had charged to their credit card account that month, she had only about twenty dollars left!

Friends, activities, gossip: Those were the things that Jessica never ran out of. But there was a constant shortage of money in her life, and it was time to start thinking of a way to change that trend.

For the time being, she had no real interest in speculating about Ginny, or Denise, or Jay, or Shelley, or anyone else. The only speculation on her mind right now was the kind that involved making money.

Denise sorted through the clothes in her closet, frowning thoughtfully and humming under her breath. In the back of her mind, she knew there was a basketball game just getting under way, and it felt a little bit strange not to be there. Since she had been dating Jay, she had never missed a home game, and very few away games, either.

The faint twinge of sadness that she felt surprised her. Going to basketball games *had* been fun. She had enjoyed the excitement of the contest, the boisterous enthusiasm of the crowd, and the intense bond between the players that was always so evident. And Jay had always sought her out and blown a kiss before he made foul shots. Yes, sometimes it really *had* been fun.

But of course that was all in the past now, she told herself firmly. Now that she had met Mike, she knew that all of that rah-rah foot-stomping and yelling was pretty juvenile. Mike was quiet and thoughtful. He was obviously the kind of guy who didn't need to show off in front of a girl. He was happy to sit and talk and just *be*. She couldn't wait to see him again on Saturday.

A glowing smile lit her face as she pulled out a light blue sweater and held it against her. She looked at herself in the mirror, wondering if blue was as becoming on her as green. She wanted Mike to see her at her best, always.

As she stood surveying her reflection the phone rang. She tossed the sweater aside and lunged across the bed, reaching for the phone. "Hello?" she asked, tossing her hair back over her shoulder.

"Hi, it's me," Ginny said.

"Hi." Denise rolled onto her back and smiled at the ceiling. "I can't believe I hardly even saw you at school today."

"I was—busy."

"Avoiding me?" Denise asked playfully as she scissored her legs in the air. "And you know perfectly well I wanted to talk to you about Mike."

"Sorry," Ginny said quietly.

"So? What did you think? Isn't he just the best?" Denise gushed. "I told you, didn't I? He's incredibly sweet and nice and—"

116

"Yes, he is," Ginny broke in.

Denise continued scissoring her legs. There was a dreamy smile on her lips. "How did we look together?"

"You looked great," Ginny said. "You always look great."

"Yeah, but as a couple?" Denise pressed.

"Den," Ginny said, "I have to ask you some—"

"Oh, come on, Ginny," Denise said. "Don't change the subject. I really want to know what you thought about Mike."

"Mike's really—really a nice guy," Ginny said. "But I just wondered, are you sure he's really your type?"

"My type?" Denise let out a tinkling laugh. "Of course he is."

"It's just that . . . do you really have that much in common?" Ginny asked.

Denise dropped her legs to the bed and rolled over onto her stomach again. "Ginny," she said in a mock scolding tone, "you know I'm just nuts about him. Are you trying to tell me something?"

There was a pause, and Denise suddenly wondered if her friend was really disappointed about the way things had turned out. After all, Ginny was the one who had started the friendship with Mike. But she had begged Ginny to tell her if she had a problem with Denise going out with Mike, and Ginny had said no.

"Listen," Denise said warmly. "You'll find someone. I know you will. You're sweet and funny and terrific, and you'll meet someone as wonderful as Mike. Don't worry."

117

"I'm not worried about that," Ginny said with a sigh.

Denise smiled. Ginny was honest. If she had any lingering unhappiness about the situation with Mike, Denise was confident her friend would have been straightforward about it.

And if Ginny did feel a bit melancholy about something, she was certainly serious about not wanting to be a wet blanket while Denise was in such an ecstatic mood.

"I have an idea," Denise said, feeling a rush of tenderness for her friend. "Why don't we do something fun tomorrow night? We can go to the movies, or to the mall, or do anything you want. Just the two of us."

"All right, if that's what you want."

"Of course I do, you dope! You're my best friend." Denise laughed.

There was a pause, and then Ginny cleared her throat. "You're my best friend, too," she said in a strained voice.

"Don't sound so sad. I didn't invite you to a wake, you know," Denise said with another laugh. "Let's decide tomorrow, OK?"

"Fine. See you tomorrow."

Denise chuckled as she hung up the phone. She was so happy that she wanted everyone else to be happy, too. She would just have to make sure that she did a good job cheering Ginny up on Friday night.

And then Saturday would come, and she'd be with Mike again.

Eleven

When Penny walked into the *Oracle* office on Friday afternoon, Elizabeth was already there, staring out the window. She turned expectantly.

"Here they are," Penny announced, dumping a sheaf of unproofed newspaper galleys on the table.

Elizabeth hurried over and paged through them. "Is it here?"

"Editorial page," Penny said. "It looks good."

Flipping to the last page, Elizabeth sat down and stared at the bold headline: "When We Are Afraid to Speak." Her essay filled two columns. She skimmed over it, rereading the words that she practically knew by heart.

"I can't believe we're doing this," she said, glancing up at Penny.

Penny shrugged. "We agreed it was the right thing to do."

"I know, but—" Elizabeth began.

The door opened, and Mr. Collins came in. Before either girl could speak, he stepped aside and Mr. Cooper came in behind him. Elizabeth's stomach plunged.

"Mr. Cooper," Penny said.

The principal shut the door and shook his head. "Elizabeth, Penny. I saw the galleys, and I have to say, I'm very surprised. At Mr. Collins, too," he added.

Penny drew a deep breath. "Mr. Cooper—"

"It was my idea," Elizabeth broke in. "Mr. Cooper, we really believe in this essay."

"Clearly," he replied dryly. "Strongly enough to betray the trust I had in both of you."

Elizabeth felt her cheeks flame. "Did you even read it?" she asked.

"That's hardly the point," Mr. Cooper said with a trace of indignation. "I thought I had made my position perfectly clear to you."

"I think they felt their responsibilities as journalists outweighed the school's concerns," Mr. Collins explained.

Mr. Cooper looked at each of them in turn. "There are some very serious allegations in this article. I do not believe that my duty to control what goes into our school paper comes under the heading of censorship," the principal said firmly. "Have you considered how parents will react when they read this? The backlash could be tremendous."

"I don't know if anyone besides the students

120

even reads our paper, to tell you the truth," Penny said.

Mr. Cooper shook his head. "All it takes is one parent picking up this paper and seeing the story and making a big stink over it. Some of our school policies and activities have already come under fire from some parent groups who think the administration is much too liberal and permissive with the students here. Starting this kind of debate is going to fan that fire even more."

"But if that happened, we could explain our position," Elizabeth pointed out hopefully. "Isn't it part of the job of any educational institution to prepare its students for the things that happen in real life, good or bad?"

"No, I'm sorry. My duty is very clear to me," Mr. Cooper insisted. "I can see what you're trying to say. But there are quite a number of people who believe that the school has no role in these kinds of family issues. I just can't open our school up to the possible backlash that this article could start. I can't let you print this in our paper. You'll have to delete the article and run the paper without it."

He looked around once more, nodded, and then left the office. In the silence, the door closed with a final, decisive thud. Elizabeth couldn't look at either Penny or Mr. Collins. She was afraid she was going to cry.

"Wow," Penny said at last.

Mr. Collins sighed heavily and pulled out a chair. "I'm sorry, girls," he said, sitting down at the conference table. "I tried. You did your best. Sometimes you just can't fight city hall."

"You've always told us that we should try, though," Elizabeth said.

"And you did try." Mr. Collins gave her a sympathetic smile. "That's what counts."

"It doesn't count enough," Penny said angrily.

"Well, I don't see what else you can do," Mr. Collins said. "We can't run the story in the paper. I can't let you do it, not now. That would be the most flagrant disregard for what Mr. Cooper has decided."

"Maybe we could have some kind of school meeting to talk about it," Elizabeth suggested.

"You're grasping at straws, Elizabeth," Mr. Collins said.

"We could stage a student protest," Penny went on, her eyes lighting up. "We could—"

"Let it go, girls," Mr. Collins urged. "Just let it go."

Elizabeth turned away. Her practical side knew that Mr. Collins was right. They had tried, and they had lost. It was time to move on.

But the emotional side of her could not take Mr. Collins's advice. She could not let it go.

Elizabeth sat down to dinner that night with a heavy heart. She ate her food as though it were an unpleasant task to get through, and answered questions automatically.

"I'm having only salad," Jessica announced, heaping half the contents of the salad bowl onto her plate. "I'm cheering tonight. It's an away game at Big Mesa."

"Are you going, Elizabeth?" Mrs. Wakefield asked. "Seeing as how you're Todd's most loyal fan."

"Yeah, I guess so," Elizabeth said vaguely.

Mr. and Mrs. Wakefield exchanged a glance. "Anything wrong between you and Todd, honey?" Mr. Wakefield asked.

She roused herself and gave her father a bright smile. "Oh, no. Not at all."

"Must be one of those temperamental writer's things she's going through," Jessica said flippantly.

Elizabeth winced. Jessica had hit closer to the mark than she knew. She put her fork down and squeezed her hands together in her lap.

"It's about this story I wrote for *The Oracle*," she began hesitantly. "Mr. Cooper handed us a gag order today."

"What?" her mother asked. "Why would he do a thing like that?"

"Oh, I know, it's that sex thing, right?" Jessica spoke up.

Mr. Wakefield choked on a mouthful of food. "What sex thing?" he asked when he could speak.

Elizabeth looked at both of her parents and sighed. "I started out to write an article about what happens when a teacher takes advantage of his authority over a student and tries to change the relationship into a personal one."

"Are you saying that's happened at school?" Mrs. Wakefield asked.

"No!" Elizabeth shook her head vehemently. "No, that's what everybody keeps jumping up and down about, but all I wanted to do was bring an important issue out into the open. As far as I know, it hasn't happened at Sweet Valley High. But it does happen at other schools, to my knowledge, and Penny and I felt that it was important enough to write an article about. Mr. Collins agreed with us, too."

She went on to explain how the article had become an essay on the ways people were pressured into keeping quiet, and finally how Mr. Cooper had insisted that the school's reputation would be at risk.

"It's not that I don't see his point," she concluded. "But I think the story was perfectly fair and factual. If you don't talk openly about controversial topics, the problem only gets worse and worse."

"That's true," their mother said quietly.

"Well, I don't know why you're so upset," Jessica said, picking at her salad. "It's just one article."

Elizabeth rolled her eyes. "The point is that Mr. Cooper never did this before," she said. "If he starts censoring us now, who's to say he won't do it again? That's no way to run a newspaper."

"Then put out your own newspaper," Jessica said bluntly. "He said it can't go in the school paper, so forget about trying to change his mind."

"What do you mean?" Elizabeth asked.

"Well, come on!" Jessica said. "You want people to read your story, right? So let them read it."

"I *could* do that," Elizabeth said thoughtfully. "I could get the story out another way."

Jessica beamed with satisfaction. "I think it's a totally cool idea. A revolutionary, counterculture, underground kind of thing. It's hot."

"First it's cool, then it's hot." Mrs. Wakefield chuckled. Then she looked at Elizabeth. "Are you willing to go that far?"

"I'm not sure," Elizabeth said truthfully.

"Mr. Cooper won't appreciate your going behind his back," Mr. Wakefield pointed out.

Elizabeth rubbed her forehead. It was hard to know what was the right thing to do. If she actually *did* put out a renegade paper, as Jessica suggested, she could easily land herself in very hot water. She had had to make many sacrifices for her fledgling career, even going so far as to appear in a silly soap opera for the chance to write a series of articles for the *Los Angeles Times*. But this action could have much more serious consequences than anything else she had ever risked.

The title of her essay, "When We Are Afraid to Speak," suddenly came to her mind. If she didn't speak out now, just because she was afraid of getting into trouble, then what was the point of wanting to be a writer at all?

"Honey, if you feel strongly enough about it, you could take the issue up with the school board," Mrs. Wakefield suggested. "There's a meeting in a couple of weeks, I think."

"No way," Jessica cried. "Strike while the iron is hot, that's what I always say."

"I've never heard you say that," Mr. Wakefield commented wryly.

Elizabeth sat up and squared her shoulders. "I think Jessica is right. Dad, can I use the copying machine in your office this weekend?"

"Elizabeth, if you're willing to go this far to defend your right to free speech, I can contribute a few hundred sheets of paper to your cause."

Jessica let out a squeal of excitement. "And I'll help you. I'll even pass them out at school."

"Maybe you should read the article before you commit yourself," Mrs. Wakefield pointed out. "You don't even know what it says."

"Oh, I don't need to," Jessica said brightly. "I trust my sister totally. She's an excellent writer, and I know it's a great article."

"Thanks." Elizabeth smiled.

"And I'll even come visit you in prison," Jessica went on with a teasing grin. "I'll bake a cake and hide a file in it, OK? Then you can bust out and run away to South America."

Elizabeth had to laugh. "You'll do *anything* if there's some kind of risk or danger involved."

"Oh, sure, you know me," Jessica said airily. "Show me a bridge and a bungee cord . . ."

"I know," Elizabeth said. "But seriously, I guess there are some risks that are worth taking, no matter what the consequences."

"Printing an underground newspaper might not be as thrilling as bungee-jumping, but it's close," Jessica said, her eyes sparkling.

"OK, we'll do it tomorrow," Elizabeth said decisively. "But right now, I have to get ready for that game. If I'm going to be hiding out in Bolivia, this might be my last basketball game for a long time."

Ginny and Denise walked into the Dairi Burger at nine o'clock. The usually crowded hangout was fairly empty for a Friday night. Ginny knew that many of the regulars were probably at the basketball game.

"Let's sit over there," Denise said, leading the way to a booth after they had bought ice cream. "Where is everyone? This place is deserted."

"Basketball game, maybe?" Ginny offered. "It's at Big Mesa tonight."

"I almost wish I'd gone," Denise said, propping her chin in her hands with a dreamy look. "Mike might have been there."

"And Jay definitely would have," Ginny said. "With Mike around, I guess basketball isn't *necessarily* so boring?"

Denise fidgeted with the paper-napkin dispenser. "I don't know."

"Don't you miss Jay?" Ginny said quietly.

Denise made a face. "Oh, come on. That relationship was so stale."

"You didn't really think so until you met Mike," Ginny said. "You two always had so much fun together."

"Yes, well . . . that's over," Denise said with a slight frown. Then she leaned forward eagerly. "Mike and I are having lunch tomorrow at the Box Tree. Don't you love it there? It's so romantic."

Ginny felt sick. "I wouldn't know. I've never been there under romantic conditions."

Denise shot a puzzled look across the table. "You're being so weird tonight. What's with you?"

"Nothing," Ginny said. She looked up as she heard someone approach their table. She hoped it would be somebody to provide a distraction, to keep her from thinking about Mike saying he wanted to break up with "Ginny." But it was just two boys who smiled admiringly at Denise and walked on past.

"I can't wait to see him," Denise went on, licking ice cream off her spoon.

"What do you two actually talk about?" Ginny asked. She looked earnestly at Denise. "I mean, I never would have expected you to like someone like him."

Denise widened her eyes. "What do you mean, you didn't think I would like someone like him? Who wouldn't?"

"I didn't mean anything," Ginny mumbled.

"Do *you* like him?" Denise asked suddenly. "Is that what's been bothering you? Are you jealous?"

Blushing, Ginny looked down at her ice cream and stirred it into a mush. "I'm not jealous," she said tiredly. "I did like him, but you're happy with him, and I wouldn't ever try to make a problem. Honest."

"You're *sure* you don't mind that he and I ended up together?" Denise pressed. "I asked you at the beginning—"

"No, I mean it," Ginny said forcefully. *Mike's already met someone new, anyway, so what's the point of being jealous of Denise?* she thought.

"Ginny," Denise said tenderly, "don't look so sad. I didn't mean for it to happen this way, but it did, and we can't go back now, right?"

Ginny looked into her friend's beautiful, sincere face and felt even worse. Denise had misinterpreted Ginny's sadness. Little did Denise know what was in store for her. And that would be Ginny's fault, too. What had seemed like such a simple deception at the start had snowballed into a disaster. She wished she could tell Denise the truth!

But she couldn't do that. Denise was going to get hurt soon enough. She deserved one more night of cheerful hope.

Twelve

Denise leaned over and flipped her long red hair over in front of her face. Through the screen of her hair, she saw the clock beside the bed: 11:45. She was meeting Mike at the Box Tree in forty-five minutes. She gave her hair several quick, hard strokes, and then stood upright again, swinging it back. She had only a few last-minute details to take care of before she was ready to go.

As she carefully brushed blush across her cheekbones, Denise thought over Ginny's comments from the night before. Was Mike really her type? she asked herself. Not in the sense that he was like the other boys she had dated, she had to admit. But that was a sign of maturity, she figured, that she was attracted to all different kinds of guys. It *had* been a bit difficult at first, trying to keep up with Mike in conversation. She wasn't good at the kind of snappy comebacks that came naturally to Ginny. But that awkwardness was the sort of thing that smoothed itself out naturally, wasn't it?

Of course, one thing about her relationship with Mike was still difficult, and would have to be resolved pretty soon. Keeping up the charade of being Ginny was getting ridiculous. If they continued to go out—and Denise was sure they would—she couldn't keep pretending to be someone else. Sooner or later, Mike would have to know the truth.

She knew she would have to be prepared for his being angry or embarrassed. But Denise was confident that what they had was strong enough to survive even that kind of upheaval.

At least, she hoped so. She couldn't anticipate Mike's reactions to things the way she had always been able to with Jay. But that was because Mike was *different*, and she knew that was one reason why she liked him so much.

Denise grabbed her handbag and ran out of the room. She couldn't wait to be with Mike.

Thirty minutes later, Denise met him outside the café. "You look great," he said.

"Thanks," Denise replied. She blushed with pleasure as she looked up into his eyes.

Mike blushed, too, and looked away. He opened the door to the café and they walked inside. Denise felt her heart do a backflip as she sat down across from him at the table. He looked as handsome as ever, although he did seem distracted.

"What's new?" she asked brightly.

"Not much. Your school creamed us at the basketball game last night," Mike told her.

"Were you there?" Denise exclaimed. "I almost went to that game. Gi—Denise wanted to go, but we went to the mall instead."

Mike dropped the roll he was buttering and blushed again. "It was a good game," he muttered.

Denise felt a twinge of uneasiness. She could kick herself for nearly saying "Ginny," and Mike's reaction made her wonder if he suspected something wasn't quite right.

"I wish I had gone. We could have sat together," she said with her most dazzling smile. "From now on, let's make it a rule to go to any Sweet Valley–Big Mesa game together. It'll be fun."

"Oh, sure, sure," Mike said. He looked around anxiously. "Where's our waitress?"

"My dad says there's never a waitress when you need one," Denise said.

Mike gave her a puzzled look. "Your dad? I thought your father died."

"I—he did," Denise said quickly. "I meant my stepfather. I call him Dad."

"I'll never be able to call Joe anything but Joe," Mike said, staring down at his menu.

Denise fiddled with the napkin in her lap. Mike seemed extremely preoccupied. He might have accepted her explanation, but it was more as though he wasn't really paying attention. She racked her brain for something to say to him. She knew he liked hiking, skiing, reading books about travel— he enjoyed a wealth of things she didn't know all that much about. She'd have to learn, she decided. This uncomfortable silence was her fault.

"Why don't we go to the beach tomorrow?" Denise said. "Do you surf?"

Mike shook his head. "No."

"Well, we can do something else, then," Denise went on, a sense of panic beginning to grip her. She knew something was wrong, but she didn't know what it was.

"I know," she went on quickly. "We could—"

"Ginny," Mike broke in. He looked at her beseechingly. "I have something to tell you."

A tight knot settled in Denise's stomach. "What?"

Mike pushed his hair out of his eyes. "Ginny, I'm really sorry, but I don't think this is going to work out."

"What?"

"I'll never forget the help you gave me," Mike went on. "I'm really, really grateful, but I don't think that's enough to base a relationship on."

"But—" Denise began. And then she couldn't go on.

Much to her surprise, she felt a tingle of relief. She didn't have to struggle anymore. It had been so much of a strain, trying to be someone else all the time, and there would have been no way to keep it up forever. Suddenly she realized that the

133

reason she'd never dated boys like Mike before was because she wasn't very comfortable with them.

"I'm really sorry," Mike said gently.

Denise smiled tenderly. "It's OK," she said. "I guess maybe I always knew this would happen."

"You're terrific, Ginny," he said. "I knew that from the first time I called you at the hotline."

"Well . . ." Denise toyed with her fork. Should she tell him the truth about who she was? If they had continued to see each other, the story would have come out eventually. But there really wasn't much point in it now, she decided. If Ginny had been interested in him, the embarrassing explanations might have been worth struggling through. As it was, it was easier just to let the matter rest.

"Let's still have our lunch together," Mike said. "As a farewell."

Denise smiled. "You know, you are a pretty terrific person," she told him sincerely. "Pretty terrific."

But not for me, she added silently.

Elizabeth stood next to the copying machine as copy after copy slid into the hopper. She pulled out a stack and tapped the edges together.

"Knock knock," came Todd's voice from the door of Mr. Wakefield's office.

Elizabeth jumped guiltily. "Oh, hi. Am I late?"

"Yes, but that's OK," Todd said, walking toward her and giving her a kiss. "You asked me to pick you up here at twelve-thirty, and I've been downstairs waiting. But since my only purpose in life is to wait on you, I was perfectly content."

"I'm really sorry," Elizabeth said with a rueful laugh. She wrapped her arms around him and gave him a fierce hug. "I don't know why you put up with me."

"Just don't push it, Wakefield." Todd looked down at her, and his brown eyes sparkled mischievously.

Elizabeth broke away as the copier finished its run. "At least these are done," she said. "My underground subversive essay."

Todd leaned against the wall and folded his arms. "Sometimes I get the sneaking suspicion that you care more about your word processor than you do about me."

"Don't say that!" Elizabeth smiled. "My word processor doesn't kiss the way you do."

"Yeah, but I bet it's better at spelling," Todd murmured, pulling her close for a kiss.

Elizabeth rested her cheek against his shoulder. She had been spending a lot of time and mental energy lately on her writing. She knew Todd was the most understanding person in the world, but maybe he was feeling a little bit neglected. She made a promise to herself that she would do something special to make it up to him.

"Are you ready to go?" he asked. "I'm starving."

"Yes. I'm all set," Elizabeth replied. She bundled up the still-warm sheets of paper and slipped them into a large manila envelope. Then she tucked the envelope into her shoulder bag and followed Todd out of the office. She carefully turned off the lights, switched on the alarm system, and locked the doors behind her.

"OK, Box Tree, here we come," Todd said, starting the engine of his car.

"Thanks," Elizabeth exclaimed. "I already know what I'm going to have."

A few moments later, they pulled into the parking lot of the café. Elizabeth silently renewed her promise to do something really nice for Todd. He was always taking her out to nice restaurants or getting her sweet little gifts. He deserved to be given a treat, too. She was going to put her mind to it and think of something really great with which to surprise him.

As they walked to the front door Denise Hadley walked out with a tall, attractive boy whom Elizabeth had never seen.

"Hi, Denise," Elizabeth said.

Denise froze. "Uh . . ."

"Say hi to Ginny for me," Elizabeth added. Then she and Todd went inside.

Denise stood staring at her hands. She could feel Mike's eyes on her.

"What did that mean?" he finally asked.

"Oh . . ." Denise waved her hand in a vague gesture. She was sure Ginny would have come up with a plausible explanation. But Denise wasn't Ginny. That was the whole point.

"I guess I have to explain," she said with a sigh.

"Yeah, I think you do," Mike agreed warily.

There was a wrought-iron bench a few paces away, and Denise led them to it. She sat down and tried to compose her thoughts.

"First of all, promise not to say anything until I'm finished," she begged.

Mike raised his eyebrows skeptically. "Can you please just tell me what's going on? I can't take a whole lot of weird stuff in my life right now."

"I know, I know." Denise drew a deep breath. "When you called the hotline and talked to Ginny, it wasn't me you were talking to. And when you wanted to meet Ginny, she asked me to meet you instead. I'm Denise."

"Then who's Denise?" Mike asked. "Who did I meet the other night?"

Denise nodded emphatically. "The other night you finally met *Ginny*."

Mike turned scarlet with embarrassment. "I don't get it. Why didn't she want to meet me herself?"

"Oh, the stupidest reason," Denise said, leaning back against the bench. "She's very shy, and she's insecure about her looks. When you told her on the phone that you were sure she was really pretty, she couldn't face you. She honestly *wanted* to meet you, but she didn't have the confidence."

Mike stared at her. "You're kidding."

"No, I'm not," Denise said. "She's incredibly shy with boys because she thinks she's unattractive."

"But she isn't!" Mike said. "I think she's *really* attractive."

"That's what I keep telling her," Denise said, staring glumly at the cars in the parking lot. Then a little ripple of curiosity made her look at Mike. She wondered if . . .

"So you're saying that when you met her the other night with me, you thought she was a lot of fun? You liked her?" Denise asked.

"Sure." Mike nodded quickly. "It was weird. Remember how I thought we had met before? That must have been because somehow I knew *she* was the girl I had talked to so much on the phone."

Denise began to smile an impish, Cupid-like smile. She scooted closer to Mike and tucked her hand in his arm. "Mike, I have an idea."

Thirteen

On Monday morning Elizabeth and Jessica arrived at school early with an armload of underground newspapers. Penny was waiting for them at the front door, and within a few minutes, a small group had gathered together to work. Todd and Enid were there, as well as John Pfeifer, Allen Walters, Olivia, and all the *Oracle* staffers. Penny had recruited them over the weekend. Elizabeth began passing out stacks of her article.

"I really appreciate your helping," she said. "But do me a favor and read the article first. I want you to know what you're getting into."

"Penny explained it all," Allen said, adjusting his glasses so that he could skim the story. "I'm behind you one hundred percent, Liz."

"Me, too," John agreed. The sports column he wrote each week wasn't a likely spot from which to explore any freedom-of-speech controversies.

139

Elizabeth was grateful that he was willing to go out on a limb with the rest of them.

"I had to write a preface to the article," Elizabeth informed Penny, "explaining Mr. Cooper's objections. I want people to know why we're handing out the article in this way."

"Let's just *plaster* the school with these!" Enid said. "By the time homeroom is over, *everyone* will have read it."

"OK. Fan out," Todd ordered. He winked at Elizabeth.

"I'm a little nervous," Olivia admitted as she riffled through a stack. "But it's exciting, too."

Allen finished reading the story and looked up. "Do you realize we're committing an act of civil disobedience?"

"That's what it's all about," Penny agreed. "Breaking the rules for a cause you believe in."

"Back to the sixties," Elizabeth said, smiling anxiously. "OK. Let's go."

For the next fifteen minutes, the group concentrated on slipping the sheets of paper into lockers, leaving piles on desks, and taping them to the bathroom mirrors. Before long, students began arriving for the day, and the halls were filled with noise and activity.

"What's this?" Elizabeth heard Maria Santelli say as she opened her locker and the folded sheet of paper fluttered out onto the floor.

All around her, Elizabeth saw people bent over the single white page, reading intently. Whenever someone passed her, she handed out another sheet. She was standing alone, in the center of the noisy hallway, when someone tapped her elbow. She turned around to see Ginny standing there, holding a copy of the article.

"I just read this," Ginny said. "This is so true. You have to be brave enough to say what you believe, even if it's hard to do."

"Believe me, I know," Elizabeth said. "Sometimes being honest feels like an incredible burden."

"It sure does." Ginny nodded as she tucked the folded article into a book. "I've always tried to be honest, but sometimes I'm afraid to speak up because I think it'll get me in trouble, or hurt me in some way—or hurt someone else."

"You can't let that stop you," Elizabeth said emphatically. "If it's important to you, you have to speak your mind. I don't know what's going to happen to me for handing out this story, but I had to do it anyway."

"Aren't you scared?" Ginny asked.

"Yes." Elizabeth managed a faint smile. "I'm terrified, actually."

Ginny looked down the hallway for a moment, and then back to Elizabeth. "You know, I've given a lot of advice on the hotline," she said. "And now I'm going to follow a little of that advice myself. Thanks."

"Good luck," Elizabeth said as Ginny walked away.

"Hey, excellent article, Elizabeth," Michael Harris said, passing her on his way to his locker. "It's

141

great that you put it out in spite of Chrome Dome." He gave her a thumbs-up sign and sauntered off.

Jessica swooped down on Elizabeth and grabbed the remaining handful of pages. "Everyone thinks this is incredible, Liz. Everyone's saying they never knew you were such a radical."

"That wasn't the point," Elizabeth said nervously.

"Don't worry," Jessica said with a cheerful smile. "People are talking about you like you're some kind of hero." She waved and hurried away.

Maybe if the whole school is behind me, I'll have some proof that the article is important, Elizabeth thought as she handed another sheet to a passing student.

Penny walked over to Elizabeth. "People are reading the story and they're really talking about it, too," she said. "From what I hear, everybody's behind you."

"I guess that counts for something," Elizabeth said nervously.

"It counts for a lot," Penny promised. "You'll see."

Elizabeth shook her head. Now that she had really stepped over the line and defied Mr. Cooper, she wanted to know as soon as possible what the fallout would be.

The homeroom bell rang and Elizabeth jumped. "I guess I'm a little worried," she admitted. "Is Mr. Cooper going to explode, or just put us in front of a firing squad?"

"I guess we'll find out right now," Penny said,

suddenly straightening her back and nodding toward the end of the hallway. "Look who's coming."

Mr. Collins was walking toward them through the milling throng of students. He beckoned urgently to Elizabeth and Penny. Elizabeth could see he had a copy of the article in his hand.

"We're wanted," he said as they fell into step next to him. They headed back the way he had come, in the direction of Mr. Cooper's office.

"Are you mad at us, Mr. Collins?" Elizabeth asked.

"Well . . . no. I'm not," he said after a moment. "I'm proud of you, actually. You've probably got more guts than I do. Nobody likes admitting that, but it doesn't make me mad at you."

"But how do you think we'll do in there?" Penny asked, nodding ahead at the door of the office.

"I think we'll survive," Mr. Collins said. "Be strong."

All of the secretaries looked up with curious expressions as Mr. Collins, Penny, and Elizabeth walked into the office. There were several copies of Elizabeth's article on the front counter.

"You can go right in," Mr. Cooper's secretary said.

As they knocked on the door Mr. Collins gave both girls an encouraging smile. "Go on," he whispered.

Elizabeth pushed open the door and stepped inside. Penny and Mr. Collins stood on either side of her.

Mr. Cooper was sitting at his desk, a copy of "When We Are Afraid to Speak" in front of him. He regarded them in stony silence for a moment. "Whose idea was this—this unauthorized publication? Mr. Collins?"

"It was the decision of the *Oracle* staff," Mr. Collins said. "But I support them completely."

Elizabeth felt a sense of unreality settle over her. For the first time in her life, she had been called to the principal's office to be reprimanded. It was a hard lesson in suffering for her convictions. And she was afraid the lesson was going to get even harder.

Mr. Cooper was clenching and unclenching his jaw. "So you decided to go ahead with this, even though I expressly forbade it."

"You told us we couldn't print it in *The Oracle*," Penny reminded him. "This is not *The Oracle*."

The principal's face became very red. "I can't tell you how shocked I am at this behavior. Penny and Elizabeth, you are two of our best students."

"Mr. Cooper," Elizabeth said calmly, "you've told me many times that I'm a credit to this school. You know I would never deliberately do anything to hurt Sweet Valley High. And I don't think that I *have* done anything to hurt this school. I strongly believe I've protected it from being hurt."

There was a long, tense silence. Mr. Cooper looked at her steadily. "Are you suggesting that my decision *was* hurtful to this school?"

Elizabeth swallowed hard. "Yes."

She heard Penny take a sharp breath. Mr. Collins was completely silent. Mr. Cooper looked down at the piece of paper on his desk, and began to shake his head slowly.

"Elizabeth," he said with a sigh, "did you think your record would get you out of trouble? Did you expect to get off easily just because I've trusted you in the past?"

Elizabeth shook her head. "No, sir. I'm prepared to take the consequences."

"You believe in this article that strongly, is that what you're saying?" he asked.

"Yes. And in my right to voice my opinion." Elizabeth clasped her hands to keep them from shaking.

Mr. Cooper sat back in his chair, looked out the window for a moment, and then nodded. "OK."

Elizabeth blinked. Penny turned and stared at her, and then at Mr. Cooper. "What?" Penny asked.

"OK," Mr. Cooper repeated. "I have to respect you both. This is a fair article, and I'm very impressed by your willingness to take the heat for your convictions."

Mr. Collins let out a long sigh of relief. "Thanks. I'm glad you see it that way."

"Not many of your peers would go out on a limb over something so abstract as a constitutional right," Mr. Cooper went on. "Most of the kids here don't even know what a constitutional right is. I have to admire the kind of maturity and judgment you two have demonstrated."

Elizabeth felt like letting out a yell of triumph—

and pure tension. It had paid to speak up for herself, even though it had been pretty frightening for a while.

"Now, in the future," Mr. Cooper went on, "let's try to formulate a school policy about stories on such controversial subjects."

Penny shook her head. "The policy has always been that the student paper is run by the students," she insisted. "Mr. Cooper, do you trust us or don't you?"

Elizabeth looked at her friend in amazement. She was impressed. That toughness was what made Penny such a good editor-in-chief.

"OK, OK!" Mr. Cooper said, throwing up his hands. "You win. I do trust you."

"And we'll never abuse that trust, I promise," Penny said seriously.

Mr. Cooper stood up and shook hands with all three of them. "Let's get to class now, OK?"

Once they were outside, Elizabeth raised her hands to her face and muffled a yelp of triumph. "Wow!" she gasped, looking at Penny. "I can't believe we did it!"

"Good work, girls," Mr. Collins said. He shook their hands. "Keep it up."

Elizabeth gave Penny a hug. It was all over, and they had won.

Ginny arrived at the Project Youth office that Monday with a lot on her mind. She *did* want to be able always to tell the truth without reservations. But that was easier said than done. At least as far as Denise was concerned.

She had called Denise a few times on Sunday to ask about her date the day before, but Denise hadn't been home. She wanted to know if Mike had actually broken up with her friend.

And Denise had been in a flighty, chattery mood throughout the entire school day. Whenever Ginny had tried to bring up the subject of Denise's lunch date with Mike, Denise had instantly gone off on a tangent. Ginny had been afraid to probe too deeply. She didn't want her friend to know how much *she* knew.

That was part of the problem, though, she realized as she sat down at the switchboard. She *should* tell Denise what she knew about Mike's feelings for her. Reading "When We Are Afraid to Speak" and talking to Elizabeth had convinced Ginny. She had to call Denise and make her listen. As soon as she got home from Project Youth, she vowed.

The moment her decision was made, a line began flashing on the switchboard. She pressed down the button.

"Project Youth. What's up?" she said.

"Hi, this is Mike," the achingly familiar voice said. "Are you by any chance the same girl I talked to on Thursday last week? About these two girls I was involved with?"

Ginny nodded, suddenly miserable. "Yes."

"Great, because I wanted to tell you what happened," he said.

147

The last thing Ginny wanted at the moment was to listen to Mike talk about how much he liked the new girl he had met. It was bad enough knowing as much as she already knew.

"Go ahead," she said, leaning back in her chair with a feeling of despair.

"I followed your advice," Mike said eagerly. "I had a date with the first girl on Saturday, and I broke up with her."

I knew it, Ginny told herself. *Maybe Denise just couldn't bear to talk about it. She didn't want to discuss it because she was so crushed.*

"Did she—was she upset?" Ginny asked. It was odd to be asking Mike how her own best friend was feeling, but there were plenty of odd things going on lately.

"Actually, not as much as I was afraid she would be," Mike said. "That was really a load off my mind. Just think, if I hadn't told her how I really felt, we'd be stuck in a relationship that didn't work for either of us."

Ginny was surprised. Denise had fallen head over heels in love with Mike at first sight. But now it looked as if it had been just a bright, brief flame instead of a steady fire.

"Well, I guess you really did the right thing, then," Ginny said.

"Definitely. And now it means that with the other girl . . ."

"Yes?" Ginny prompted automatically.

"Now I can ask her out with a clear conscience," Mike concluded triumphantly.

Ginny gulped hard. She didn't want it to hurt,

but it did. A lot. Move on, look toward the future—it was good advice, but she couldn't follow it. She could only think of what might have been between them. And now it was much too late.

"That's great," she whispered, feeling absolutely miserable. She didn't want him to talk about it anymore. She thought she might have to turn the call over to someone else.

"Yeah, I'm really glad," Mike went on. "And you know what? I'm going to ask her to go out with me tonight!"

Fourteen

"Did you hear what I said?" Mike asked after a pause. "I'm asking her out tonight."

Ginny covered the mouthpiece of her headset while she drew a long, shaky breath. "Yes. I heard you."

"She's a terrific girl. She's funny, smart, really kind."

Ginny leaned her forehead against her hand. Why did he have to go on like this?

"She's pretty, too," Mike went on. "I see her in my imagination all the time."

That was the last straw. "I—I have to go," she said with difficulty. "I'm happy for you, but I really have to go."

She ripped the headset off as she hung up. "I'll be right back," she mumbled to the other counselors.

Nearly blinded by hurt and sadness, Ginny wrenched open the door and stumbled out into the hall. She closed her eyes and leaned against the wall, hearing the memory of Mike's voice in her mind.

"So, where should we go tonight?" Mike asked.

"I don't know," Ginny said with a sigh. "Don't ask me."

Then her eyes flew open and she spun around. Mike was standing behind her, a mischievous grin on his face.

"What—?" she asked, thunderstruck.

He dug his hands into his pockets. "I was calling from over there," he said, nodding toward the pay phone at the end of the hallway.

Ginny pressed her back against the wall and tried to steady herself. What was going on?

"Denise told me everything on Saturday," Mike continued. "And when she said you were here last Thursday, I figured out that it was you I talked to. I was describing *you*, you dope. You're the 'new girl.' "

"But—" Ginny shook her head. "You said she was really pretty."

"That's right. I did," Mike agreed.

Ginny was suddenly afraid she was going to burst into tears. She couldn't believe how happy she was. It was like a dream.

"Listen," he went on, stepping closer and gently taking one of her hands in his. "Let's start from the beginning, OK?"

"OK," Ginny whispered. His hand was warm around hers.

"My name is Mike," he said, his eyes twinkling. "And you are . . . ?"

She grinned bashfully. "Ginny. Pleased to meet you, Mike."

"Ginny? You're *sure* about that?" he asked doubtfully. "You're the same girl I talked to on the phone all those times?"

Laughing, Ginny nodded. "Honest."

"Good word," Mike said. "Let's try to be totally honest with each other from now on, OK?"

"OK," she agreed.

They smiled at each other, and Ginny thought she had never been so glad in all her life. Finally, she had to break eye contact so that she didn't completely melt.

"Did Denise cook this up?" she asked at last. "I wondered if she was deliberately avoiding me."

Mike nodded. "She thinks you're pretty terrific," he said. "When I told her how much I liked you, she couldn't wait to help me out with a scheme."

Ginny laughed. Denise had been trying for ages to get Ginny together with a boy she liked. And now she had finally succeeded. The only sad thing was that they wouldn't be able to have that double date that Denise had always pined for. Not now that Denise had broken up with Jay.

"So, where should we go tonight?" she asked, looking back at Mike shyly.

He grinned. "How about—"

"The Lucky Duck?" she broke in.

"Exactly." Mike smiled at her. "Can I call you at home later? I can't keep calling you on the hotline, you know."

Ginny wrote her phone number on a slip of

paper she had in her pocket and handed it to him. Then she held her breath while he walked to the door. As he opened it he turned and waved, and then stepped outside. When the door shut behind him, Ginny let out a scream of pure joy.

"What's wrong?" Kathy asked, running out into the hall.

Ginny apologized quickly. "It's nothing. But I was just thinking—this hotline really lives up to its name."

Kathy gave her a puzzled look and Ginny went back in to the switchboard. She had a phone call to make herself. She had to tell Denise how glad she was that they were best friends.

Jessica hung up the phone in the kitchen and began to set the table for dinner. "You won't believe this," she said to Elizabeth.

"What?" Elizabeth was making salad dressing, and she shook the ingredients together in a bottle as she looked over at her twin.

"That was Lila," Jessica said, putting plates on the table. "She said she was just at the Dairi Burger, and you'll never guess which two people were there together."

"Lady Macbeth and Frankenstein's monster?"

Jessica sent Elizabeth a withering glance. "No. Denise Hadley and Jay McGuire. They got back together today."

Elizabeth smiled. "Oh. That's great."

"Greetings, earthlings," Mr. Wakefield said, walking in the back door. He kissed Elizabeth's cheek and picked a piece of lettuce out of the salad bowl. "Mom home yet?"

Jessica cocked her head toward the front of the house. "I think I just heard her car."

In moments, the family was gathered together in the kitchen, getting dinner ready and filling each other in on their news. When it was finally time to sit down to eat, Mrs. Wakefield looked at Elizabeth expectantly.

"So? What happened with the article?"

"Big success, no problem," Jessica put in before Elizabeth could speak. "School hero, et cetera."

"Let's hear it from Elizabeth," their father suggested.

Elizabeth took a sip of milk. "Well," she said, "At first Mr. Cooper was pretty upset. He raked me and Penny and Mr. Collins over the coals. But Penny and I stood up for our rights, and Mr. Cooper finally accepted the fact that it is unethical for him to censor us."

"And Mr. Collins?" their mother asked.

"He was great," Elizabeth said with a smile. "When this whole thing started, he was pretty unsure about whether I should go ahead. But he backed me up completely. He's the best."

Mr. Wakefield nodded judiciously. "He's that rare, old-fashioned thing—a good teacher."

"We're proud of you, sweetie," Mrs. Wakefield said, giving Elizabeth's hand a squeeze.